A NOVEL

MICHAEL LANDWEBER

coffeetownpress

Seattle, WA

coffeetownpress

Coffeetown Press
PO Box 70515
Seattle, WA 98127

For more information go to: www.coffeetownpress.com
mikelandweber.com

Cover design by Sabrina Sun

ISBN: 978-1-60381-166-8 (Trade Paper)
ISBN: 978-1-60381-167-5 (eBook)

Library of Congress Control Number: 2013940935

Printed in the United States of America

ACKNOWLEDGMENTS

MANY THANKS TO Catherine, Jennifer, Emily and the rest of the Coffeetown team for their hard work on *We*. It is a better book because of them.

I have been lucky to have so many great teachers in my life. In particular, thanks to Mrs. Marten (1st-3rd grade), Mrs. Meanwell (8th grade) and Mrs. Palmer (high school), who were all instrumental in helping me learn how to write.

I am also indebted to my friends from the Montgomery Country group for getting me writing short stories again (which led to a return to novels) and the folks at Purgatory who made me realize that no matter what I'm going through as a writer, someone else is experiencing the same thing.

My family has always been incredibly supportive of my writing. Sharon and David provided me with insights on psychology and cumin-free food. Jon, my partner in all things screenplay, has made me a better writer. And, of course, thanks to my parents, without whose love and encouragement I never would have accomplished any of this.

Finally, this book is for Gillian for always believing in me and for Josh and Maya for being awesome.

ONE

THE PANIC CAME on quickly, just as it always does. One moment, I am fine. Then it grips me and squeezes. Sometimes my upper arm, sometimes my gut, occasionally icy fingers clutching my throat. Always tight and angry.

Roger encouraged me to focus on the physical during an episode. That's what he called them. Episodes. I never let him use his clinical speak on me—except when I needed to cling to it. *You are not my analyst*, my favorite phrase. Except when he is.

He's gone now, though. Not gone gone, but gone enough. No longer my lover. Not here to help me.

Focus.

I tried to pinpoint where the fear held me. But it was elusive. I knew it was there. It had to be. The hyperventilation. The pounding heart. The wooziness. All the symptoms that I'd been taught to identify and then vanquish.

I found nothing.

And yet, clearly, panic.

I had experienced panic attacks before. Not infrequently. I even panicked in my dreams.

This had to be a dream.

Focus.

I stood in front of a refrigerator staring at a picture drawn by a child. An adult—certainly a teacher—had written "This is my family" at the top. In the bottom left corner, in the same teacher's hand, "Ben, age 3."

Even without reading my name, I recognized the picture. It had graced our refrigerator door for nearly a decade before I finally pulled it down and stuffed it in the trash, long after it had lost all meaning and was merely a remnant of a time we had all forgotten.

A time when we were still a family.

But here it was, at eye level before me. There were my mother and father in their stick figure glory, with long and short hair respectively. I had drawn my father in a top hat and bow tie, though I had never seen him wear either. My older sister Sara stood next to my mother, just an eyebrow shorter but with the same burnt ochre hair. Then the two boys, me and Charles. Of course, my brother should have stood next to Sara, approximately the same height. That was his rightful place in the birth order. But that stick figure had two unsteady letters written under it—M E. Charles was the tiny boy at the end of the line, a full three inches shorter than the rest of us. If I had been a prodigy, which of course I wasn't in any way, then maybe it could have been said that I was playing with perspective, drawing my brother as if he stood a football field behind us. But I had just made him short and me tall and usurped his rightful place as the middle child. Though to be honest, with seven years between us, I often felt as if Charles was the youngest child and I was of a different generation.

I had briefly forgotten the panic, distracted by the anachronistic picture that could not possibly still exist nearly thirty years after being sent to a landfill. Construction paper had to be biodegradable.

Whenever Roger told me to focus, he meant distract myself.

It was true that sometimes a diversion would make the panic dissipate, without the usual need to complete some random task like turning on and off the lights or checking the stove or scrubbing that discoloration on the ceiling of our apartment. No, not *our* apartment anymore—*my* apartment.

The stain on the ceiling. The memory of it flowed through me, a torrent. It had to be removed, whatever it was. Leaking water from the apartment above, most likely. This attack had happened in the recent past. Yesterday, or maybe the day before—I couldn't quite recall. But it was clear in my memory that the panic had locked itself around my thighs, squeezing them so that I could feel the thumping of the blood pulsing through my femoral arteries. The tension did not start to ebb until I was up on that step stool, which was at least a foot too short for the task, rubber gloves on, Windex and toilet brush in hand, stretching for the corner of the living room ceiling, just out of reach. Reaching, then falling. Then, pain. Not like the panic. Actual searing pain in my head and neck and shoulders. I believed there was blood on the floor, but everything was upside down. There was no balance left in the world. It ended with the face of Mr. Colson, my next door neighbor, thank god we had traded keys, bending close, his lips moving, words, I heard a loud crash, they're coming, just relax. Then, hands grabbing me, something tight around my mouth and nose, rolling out of the apartment, sirens and lights. Then … I don't know.

Here.

Focus.

A poodle-shaped magnet bonded the picture to the refrigerator just over three feet above the ground. I thought I was on my knees, but looking down, I found my feet stuffed into a pair of impossibly small Keds sneakers, lightly used and blindingly white. Someone had written BEN in thick black magic marker on the toes of each shoe, pointing up at me.

My mother used to do that. I often wondered if she thought I might forget my own name.

My hands—void of hair, never scarred, unblemished, soft, with fingers like smooth marsh reeds—rose before me.

Those are not mine, I thought. *This is not me.*

I'd been taken to a hospital after the fall. I was now sure of that, though any details eluded me. They must have me pumped up on drugs. This had to be a hallucination. Because it did not feel like a dream. Not exactly. I was immersed. This felt vivid and real. Intense and uncomfortable.

I glanced up. Had I done that? I wasn't sure. Above me loomed the refrigerator, covered with more cheerful magnets and juvenile works of art collecting on it like barnacles. This was my old kitchen on Sycamore Street.

The urge arrived. *Remove everything from the front of the refrigerator. Now.* That was the task.

But my arms couldn't move. That wasn't right. They were not mine. My eyes closed. Wrong again. The eyes of this child closed. The refrigerator, the kitchen, the task—gone. I was grateful for the darkness. At least momentarily. Then, I realized that my eyes were in fact open. When my childhood kitchen disappeared, I no longer felt encased in the body of that child, but instead occupied myself again. The forty-year-old body all too familiar to me. But not in the hospital. Somewhere completely foreign—my first thought was that I was in a cave. The darkness was not complete. Shadows appeared, gradations of black. My eyes adjusted to this new place. I held my hands— they were my hands again—in front of my face. They were light, as was all of me, as if I was only a portion of my true self, incoherent. I struggled to rationalize my circumstances and failed. But the panic was blessedly gone. For now.

It was a cave. As the light filtered through, I could see that now. My back pressed into the wall behind me, which felt like foam, giving a little as I tensed. I was wrong, the panic was still with me, but quiet, as thoroughly confused as I was.

Focus.

I could sense that there were spaces beyond this place where I cowered. There was room to roam here and that scared me even more. I only wanted to sit still and wait for it to pass. This place was too full of possibility.

I felt the presence of others in the cave. Watching me, considering me. Two of them, one large and menacing, the other small and thoughtful. I was not alone. I saw nothing, yet was certain they were behind me. No, that wasn't possible—my back was against a wall.

I leapt to my feet, spinning around. Nothing there. Off to the side. What was that? It moved. *They* moved. I caught a glimpse of something in my peripheral vision. As I turned, dizzying myself, the things stayed just out of my sight. They were faster than I could ever be. My own rapid movement overwhelmed me. I tumbled over, landing hard, retching.

Not a dream or a hallucination or a vision or a memory. This felt more real than anything had for some time. All I wanted was for it to end.

Warm breath on the back of my neck. Something sniffed my hair in short pungent bursts. I tried to close my eyes and found that I couldn't.

"Lance! Oh god, it's happening again." The voice was alarmed, shrill. It echoed around me in the cave, but it came from somewhere outside it. "Binky, honey, can you hear me?"

That voice, so familiar, lost for so long.

"Calm down, Charlotte. Please." A second voice, also known to me, deep and frustrated. It spoke again, in a tone that was different but no less angry. "Benedict. Answer your mother's question."

The eyes opened again—the eyes of that child. Relief swept over me. I was ecstatic to be out of that cave and back in the kitchen. Yet, even then, in those first few moments, I was starting to suspect that I existed in both places simultaneously, that the two could not be separated from each other. But I chose to focus on what I could see, adjusting again from dark to light.

I needed to stay calm, to ride out this trip. I wished Roger was here to tell me to focus. But I was alone.

TWO

.

GENTLE, FIRM HANDS took me by the elbows and turned me away from the refrigerator. I now faced into the kitchen. They stood before me. Their words sounded clearer, crisper than any I had heard in years. And now I realized that everything around me indeed existed. My parents—yes, they were my parents—breathed, she with a shallowness that betrayed the tears threatening to surface and he with a steadiness that signified profound detachment. Her polyester pants rustled like dead leaves as she crouched before me. His teeth clicked.

"Binky? Binky, come on, honey."

And there she was, my mother, kneeling down to my height, the features of her face so sharp that they cut my eyes. His eyes. Our eyes. My mother's sadness drowned me, filled me, cut off all air. I wanted to breathe, but these tiny little lungs in this tiny little body could not possibly sustain me. I could hardly find the air they drew in, despite their best efforts. I had never seen a face as clearly as this one before me, and the reality of it shredded my memories of my mother. I wanted to howl in pain at the loss. For twenty years, I had imagined her old and wrinkled, as she should have been to me, when in truth this woman was young, and the last time I had seen her, a decade later, she had still been young. I had betrayed myself, allowing my imagination to age her.

But here she was. Her hand reached for my cheek. I knew when it touched me I would implode, matter negated by anti-matter, that I would cease to exist. And I was right, for as her fingers brushed my skin, I felt my cells dissolve, the skin, the muscle, the marrow, all rendered insubstantial by her mere existence.

My father's voice startled me with its force.

"That's enough. He's fine."

He towered over me, blocking out the sun. I was overwhelmed by the need for his approval. It terrified me that his reassurance that everything was okay somehow rendered the situation horribly wrong.

These thoughts pulled me out of the depths where my mother's love sustained me and deposited me on the shore where I was fully exposed to the deadly elements of my father's expectations and disappointments.

My reaction made no sense. These people held no power over me. Not anymore. It frustrated Roger to no end when he tried to get me to talk about my family.

"They're dead to me," I would say.

And he would respond, "Family never leaves you," countering my petulance with a Hallmark platitude.

Of course, he was wrong. My family had left. One at a time and each in their own way.

I forced my mind to recall my father as an old man. The last time I had seen him, just before I ended up in the hospital, he had been bent and desperate and gray. I gave him money and sent him on his way. He was no threat to me. My father was a failure. That is the man I knew. I tried to take pleasure in having bested him at his own profession. He toiled away at the base of the ladder at his small town law firm, while I excelled at corporate law in Manhattan, my task-oriented nature perfectly suited to those massive cases. But I never could gloat; it was too tiring.

But now there was another man, a different father, in front of me, teeth clicking, waiting for me to do something. Tensed, I could feel the danger in the combination of his strength and my weakness. I reminded myself that he was a timid man. There was no threat here. But I cowered before his animus. Until my mother took my hand.

"Come on, Binky," she said. "We've got to go soon."

In her grasp, my fingers warmed from within as if my knuckles were tiny glowing coals. I wanted to walk with her, but I could not move. I was aware of how light I was. My feet were rooted to the ground. I feared that if I took a step, I would float away from her, a lost balloon disappearing forever into the suburban blue sky that matched the wallpaper. I figured I was one hundred and fifty pounds lighter in this kitchen than I was in that hospital bed. I willed my limbs and torso to fill with the molten lead that had congealed inside my body over the decades, the concrete that had set in my adult bones and tethered me to those starched sheets.

And then I was flying. My fears—my hopes—had been realized. Gravity had no hold on me.

My mother had lifted me into her arms and pressed me to her chest. I fit perfectly there, my face peering over her shoulder as she carried me from the kitchen.

"Charlotte," my father called after her. "We weren't going to carry him anymore."

"We're late," she said.

Up here at the appropriate height, I could see him for who he was. Tears clouded my eyes.

I realized that everything I felt was truer and deeper than it would ever be again. The emotions wrapped around me like a series of blankets, each one not a part of me, but affecting my perception of the world. I was not in control.

Even through the salty film, I could see perfectly. No need for contacts or glasses anymore. Words embroidered on the wall—"This hearth is a home"—and on the cereal boxes on the table—"Fortified for your goodness"—were legible from any distance. Things remembered—a dish here, a glass there—and things forgotten—the stand-up mixer. It was only as my eyes skittered around the room that I saw my brother sitting at the kitchen table, a pile of toast in front of him. Charles watched me leave the room in the arms of our mother. He brushed a strand of jet black hair, so different from the rest of ours, off his forehead, scratched at his acne-scarred cheeks, lifted a piece of jam slathered toast toward his braces-encrusted teeth and locked me in an angry glare.

But I didn't care. I was flying. My mother carried me only a few feet to the hall bathroom. I never wanted her to put me down. But she did.

"Brush your teeth now. Just like we practiced. Up and down. Left and right. Inside and out."

She smiled at me and I shattered anew.

I must get a handle on my emotions, I thought. *I must control myself. If this is real, I must be able to take control.*

The bathroom was yellow with tiny shells lining the wallpaper trim. The soap dish was also shell-shaped as were the decorative soaps, five scallops in a jumble. The only thing that clashed in this bathroom was a neon blue toothbrush I assumed was mine. But instead of the toothbrush, Binky took a soap and placed it on the ledge behind the sink. Then, a second and a third, all in a perfect row, neatly fanning out toward the mirror. My mother noticed when he went for the fourth.

"You don't need to do that," she said. "You need to brush."

I heard the footsteps in the hall. My father lingered there and she went out to talk to him. The water crashed out of the tap like a waterfall. I tried to hear my parents' conversation, struggling to make out the words. The bristles of the toothbrush scraping enamel sounded like a hurricane blowing through a subdivision, splintering everything in its path.

"We have an appointment next week." My father's voice.

"I know. Just call and see if we can move it up."

"Why can't you call?" he said.

"It's hard at the store. You've got—"

"Time?" Irritation rising. "Like I have nothing to do?"

"I know you're working," she said. "Just … can you call? Please."

I spit into the sink and watched the foaminess of the toothpaste dissolve into the water. I could hear the bubbles pop and fizz. I could feel them die.

Roger had colleagues who worked with children. At dinner parties, they always said that their clients felt things differently than adults. I never believed them. Until now.

The toothpaste gel coated my tongue, like a thick layer of Vaseline.

"Fine," he said, "I'll call. Where's the number?"

"Dr. Millard's card is tacked to the board," she said. She knew he knew where the number was and he knew she knew. "Right next to the calendar."

I considered myself in the mirror. It was me. Me *then*. I had seen pictures of my young self, but I always had trouble associating them with myself as an adult. I understood what I looked like at that age, but none of my memories involve looking in the mirror.

My own thinness alarmed me. Although I don't think I wanted them to, my twig-like fingers ran over my bony chest, scaling over the jut of my collarbone to come to rest on the shoulder blade that strained against my skin. There was so little of me—so little to me. No wonder my parents sounded worried.

But the concern was unfounded. I ran a palm over my arm and felt the tautness, the give. My limbs all swiveled within their joints easily, without pain, well oiled and smooth. The heart that beat within me, steady and firm, was as of yet unclogged by time and cholesterol. There was no weariness in my muscles, no deterioration in my liver. Not yet. Despite my apparent frailty, I felt nothing but health in my being. And youth. I watched my lips stretch outward into a smile and it carried me away as surely as the arms of my mother.

The soaps ... Quickly, those little fingers snatched the last two and spaced them perfectly in line with the others.

Creaks on the floorboards over my head. Gentle thuds on the stairs. Someone was coming down.

Sara.

I ran from the bathroom. Past my mother, who I realized had been standing in the hallway, watching me. I heard Sara's voice.

"Bye, Mom, Dad. See you later!"

"What about breakfast?" my father called from the kitchen.

I was too late. I caught only a glimpse of her ponytail and her pink fingernails as she pulled the door shut behind her. Continuing my momentum, I bounded into the living room, delighted at my ability to launch myself into the air toward the couch, coming to a stop after two bounces on the cushions. I peered out the window as Sara got into Xavier Pascal's car. I touched the glass, unconcerned about fingerprints, and was seized by the feeling that I would never see her again.

Where am I? When am I?

Suddenly, nothing was more important.

Outside everything was green. There were flowers. I was wearing shorts and a T-shirt. But I was going to school. Late spring, early summer. All of those clues mattered. The picture on the refrigerator. The work of a three-year-old. But I am too big. Not that young.

Xavier's car pulled away from the curb, ferrying my sister off to school. Had he dated Sara when I was six?

No. He dated Sara when I was seven. I had to be five or even six, anything but seven.

That would make it 1977. The year that three boys, ranging

from seventeen to twenty-one years of age, raped my sister on a clear Thursday night. The oldest assailant was Ezekiel Pascal, Xavier's older brother. Sara called them X and Z. She joked that they needed a sister named Yolanda. X, Y, Z—that would be perfect.

Frozen there on the couch, I heard her say it again and I saw her face light up, that face I missed so desperately. I had let her walk out the door.

I felt the bile rise into my esophagus. *I don't belong here. I can't be here. Not again. Not here. Not now.*

My head jerked around and I again suspected that I was not in control of this body. There was someone else. We looked at the foyer, and I remembered the night they'd brought her home.

There was a little lip at the threshold of our front door—who knew if it was an architectural quirk or the work of a lousy contractor? But we all trained ourselves to step higher when coming inside. That night, Sara tripped as she entered the house. The cop behind her, a squat woman with bristly hair, grabbed her arm to keep her steady then followed her into the foyer. At first, sitting up on my perch at the top of the stairs, I thought the cop had pushed her. It was hardly a memorable moment except to a child of seven who knew his sister would normally never forget about that ridge at the front door. I had seen Sara distracted, but this was different. She had become a stranger here, in her own house, in her own skin.

There were two cops present that night. Once Sara and the policewoman had cleared the threshold, the second cop—an angry-looking man, middle-aged and no doubt thinking of his own daughter—blocked the doorway itself. There was no sound save for the clipped breathing of my mother, trying to quell a panic attack. The words had already been spoken. The cops had called ahead to let my parents know that they were en route with their broken daughter. There would be more words, once they all sat down in the living room, as the four adults tried to coax my struck-mute sister to tell her horrible story. But I was not there to listen to all that. I only saw the silence.

Sara had a wool blanket draped over her shoulders. I could not see her hands beneath it, but I knew that they gripped the scratchy fibers tight across her breasts. Tattered fragments of her spangled top, the one that reminded me of confetti, stuck out from the grayish brown blanket like ruined remnants from the Fourth of July. I had watched Sara get ready to go out that night, but later I could not summon any memories of what she had looked like ... before ...

My mother stood just behind my father, less than an arm's length away. She could have touched him, but did not. My father's arms were crossed and unavailable. The tall cop, the angry father, fists clenched at his side, refused to make eye contact with either of them. Only the policewoman touched my sister, now placing the same hand that had steadied her fall on her shoulder. An anchor, ballast.

It was only me on the stairs that night. My brother, Charles, must have been in his room, alone and apart as always, listening to his stereo through those massive headphones. He would not have heard them arrive. He would not know what had happened.

Sara looked up at me. It was not my sister. It was someone else. Someone new. Someone who scared me. I almost bolted for the safety of my room right then, but those new eyes, Sara's new eyes, pleaded with me to stay. Not to stay on the stairs. But to stay the same. To remain unchanged. To help her find her way back to where we had been just a few hours earlier.

In the foyer on Sycamore Street, the policewoman's hand moved down to an innocuous point between my sister's shoulder blades. Yet the touch, the movement, caused my sister to flinch, which in turn caused a ripple through my father, my mother, the cop by the door, me. We all felt what she felt and wished it could be otherwise.

The adults and my sister flowed into the other room, away

from me. There, the details would become known. There, things would change without me.

The terrible memory stopped there, and I was back in the present, *Binky's* present, whenever that might be.

I was running into the kitchen. There was a counter by the kitchen door piled high with papers, things that needed to be done or organized or dealt with by the adults of the house. Above those piles, my mother had tacked a calendar, an erasable sheet of plastic that listed all our activities. My mother marked time by X'ing out the days that had passed.

I stared at the calendar. The heading at the top: May/June 1977, scribbled in my mother's hand. My eyes climbed over the crossed off days, scaling the X's like a jungle gym, until I finally arrived at Monday, June 6. Three days until Thursday, June 9.

The day of my sister's rape.

I wanted to scream. To tell my parents what was going to happen. But I couldn't. I had no voice. No, that's not true. I had a voice. I was screaming at the top of my lungs, angry and scared, deep inside that cave. I could hear my own voice echo there, as in a soundproof chamber. But the kitchen was silent. The boy, Binky, stared at the calendar, having fallen back into a fugue state. I knew my father and mother and brother were watching me again.

It had not happened yet. I couldn't go through that again. I couldn't watch it happen again.

The years of revelations and evidence jumbled through my thoughts, images and feelings beyond the experience or comprehension of this young person. Details from the trial, conversations with Sara, recriminations and tragedy, the detritus of the aftermath.

I felt something quiver. The world around me shook with it. *Stop it. Please.*

The voice was so quiet I did not notice it at first.

Stop it.

That voice, that reedy, childish, familiar voice, was inside the cave with me.

But all I could see was the kitchen. Inside, I felt him and heard him, but I was distracted by the world outside us.

Inside that cave, I spoke with my voice.

Close your eyes, I said. *So I can see you.*

Binky did as he was told. The kitchen disappeared. I was in the cave again, though I realized now that I had never left it. My eyes adjusted almost immediately this time. Everything was lighter than before, less imposing, softer.

Binky stood across the cave floor. The boy in the mirror. It was his voice, his body.

I was seven.

No, not I. I remained forty-two. *He* was seven.

He, me, us.

We considered each other warily.

What is happening? I said.

Immediately, I regretted my words. His small features contracted into a frown. This boy had been expecting me to *answer* that question, not ask it. We were both lost. I could sense others, deeper in the shadows, but this boy, this fragile child, was holding them at bay.

I took a step forward. He sprinted toward the wall.

No, wait.

But the boy, Binky, ran through the barrier and was gone. I was alone again. I considered following, believing that I too could pass through what seemed solid.

But I never had the chance. Binky's eyes were open again. I was flooded by the kitchen. He started to cry, wounding our mother and pushing our father further away.

Not he. *We.*

We cried.

We were not alone, and together we let our mother lead us to the car. She buckled our seatbelt and kissed our forehead. Charles piled into the seat next to us, awkwardly trying to pull his heavy backpack in with him. He had been born unfortunate and graceless. We grounded ourselves in the honey brown hair of our mother's head as she turned on the car and backed out of the driveway.

We breathed together, and separately considered our next steps. Our situation, our predicament. Me and Binky. Together.

THREE

WE RODE IN silence. My mind wandered despite the circumstances. Noises that normally would have gone unnoticed intruded. The car growled and grumbled, the engine burping and sputtering and dreaming of technology yet to be invented. The seat vibrated beneath Binky, the upholstery scraping at his bare legs, sending an uncomfortable hum through our teeth. Binky stared out the window and I watched my hometown pass by as we navigated its mostly familiar streets.

I could feel him nearby, my younger self, lurking in the murky depths, hiding and watching, waiting.

It was not until years after Sara's suicide that I'd decided to research what had happened that night for myself. My parents shielded me from the details, even after Sara died, one thousand miles away from us, alone at college, without so much as a note.

Once, during an argument with Roger, he told me that I had never confronted my feelings about my sister. In rebuttal, I told him about digging up the newspaper stories and the court records. How I read the transcripts of the testimony and interviewed the lawyers on both sides. It was simple, gaining access. All I had to do was say that my sister had killed herself and that I was trying to find closure. Everyone opened up, purging themselves of the guilt, repenting for whatever sins they imagined they had committed. Roger listened and calmly—he was always calm when he knew he was right, so smug—told me that I hadn't dealt with my *feelings* about the rape. I remember it clearly—his use of the word "feelings." Like he owned them. Like he had the right. He said I had merely cloaked myself in the construct of an investigative journalist. I walked out on him and didn't come home, refusing to take his phone calls, until finally he tracked me down and apologized and agreed not to bring the subject up again.

In the car, Binky turned away from the window. He looked at our mother, his arms tensed, his knees locked and legs braced against the front seat.

The car lurched to a stop at the high school. Charles got out and we started rolling again.

Sara had not consented, that much was clear from the evidence. Her clothing was ripped off of her. She struggled as they held her down. The first two—Z and Anthony Righetti—had scratches on their faces and arms. At some point she had given up. The third boy—Jackson—was unscathed, and tried unsuccessfully to inject that into his defense. Where the jury ultimately saw despair, the defense argued capitulation. But the examination proved his undoing. Like the others, he had left pieces of himself embedded in her—his hair on her clothing, his skin under her fingernails, his sperm floundering inside. One of the lawyers I talked to mentioned that it was a miracle that she didn't get pregnant. He meant it to be a silver lining, speaking the words mere seconds before recalling that Sara was dead and I was her brother.

There were other things I knew. They'd grabbed her at the party that Thursday night. She was drunk or stoned or both. No one helped her.

I have had the nightmares both awake and asleep. I am there with her at the park. I witness the attack and I want to save her, but I am unable to do anything. I can only watch.

How dare Roger tell me I hadn't dealt with it? I dealt with it every day. And now, here I was again, doomed to relive the source of my nightmares.

Sitting in the car, as we pulled up in front of the elementary school, I was—in my thoughts—in the park, watching her get raped. Standing there, alone, helpless.

The world disappeared in a squall of blinding white light. The air was sucked away from me, crumpling my body in on itself, a tin can in a depressurized cabin.

I struggled to speak to him.

It hurts, I said, sucking the words through broken teeth.

We were back in the cave. I could not see him—I saw nothing. But I knew he was there, somewhere, crushing me.

Stop, I said.

The pressure eased slightly. I felt my limbs reinflate. The pain subsided.

You stop!

Binky was petulant and firm. I didn't know what I had done.

Why are you hurting her?

Binky's voice pleaded with me. All around me. Within me. The cave came into focus. I was there alone, though I felt him, and others, nearby.

Stop hurting Sara. Please.

I'm not hurting her, I said. *I would never …*

HE LIES. WE SAW.

I scrambled away from this new voice, also unseen but ever-present. Though this one, a shredding growl, seemed to occupy the ground below me, the air around, the very marrow in my bones. I was paralyzed, needing to flee but unable to do so.

A third voice calmed the second.

Shh, shh, it's okay. Let us leave them be.

I felt the two voices vacate the space, leaving me alone with Binky once again.

Stop hurting her.

I had done something. But I had done nothing. I was only sitting here thinking.

Thinking, remembering, sharing.

Could he read my mind? Was I nothing but an open book to him? I was inside Binky. Could it be that he was also inside me? I knew next to nothing about this arrangement, this fusing of our selves, but I had assumed that my thoughts, my memories, remained only mine.

I didn't hurt her, I said. *She was hurt.*

That was the wrong answer. Binky shivered and the world that surrounded us went cold. I sensed us slowing down, fossilizing.

There was danger here. Not the external danger of the other voices. No, this was something deeper, more elemental, like picking at a scab until it stings and opens and bleeds and you realize that you hold the ultimate power to hurt yourself.

I decided I needed to be more careful. I was not free to think. Not until I understood more. I had to compartmentalize, to shut parts of myself off from the rest. I believed that I could hide things from him.

Shh, shh, it's okay, I said, mimicking the tone the third voice had used. *It's okay. That wasn't real. Like a movie.*

Where's Sara?

Sara is at school. She's okay. Shhhhhh.

And the caverns we shared thawed. We calmed.

Like a movie.

Yes, yes, I said. *Just like that.*

I believed it too, that everything I knew about my sister's rape was in fact fictional. It *was* a movie. Events that had not passed yet. The future to come. I found comfort there with Binky.

Binky opened his eyes when our mother came around to

the door. Without looking at us, she tapped on the window, a warning or a courtesy, I couldn't tell. She opened the door and leaned across my small frame to undo the seatbelt. Her hair tickled my face and my arm. It was longer than I remembered. So vivid, each strand before my eyes, and I realized that it was still its natural color rather than the alternating gray and bottled white blonde of my teenage years.

Behind her, Jefferson Elementary School stretched away from us. The single-story building was exactly as I remembered it, covered with puce panels and probably filled with asbestos.

"Come on, Binky," she said. "Time for school."

Her words were tinged with sadness.

"I don't want to!"

The voice surprised me, issuing so close within, stronger and louder than I imagined. I was momentarily shocked when I realized that in the short time I had been with him, Binky had not spoken aloud, not a word. I was dragged along on a wave of emotion as Binky lunged for my mother, wrapping his arms tight around her. My mother pulled back and gave in at the same time. I could feel her melt and tense up. Binky's love and need swallowed us all.

"Come on, honey," she said, trying to pull back.

But he clung to her. Unwittingly, she pulled us out of the car. We stumbled to the ground, our fall impeded only by my mother's knee. I felt her wince and knew that the impact had hurt. But Binky did not care. Now that she was down at his level, he could possess her completely and he pressed the length of his body into her.

"I want you to stay," he said.

That was *our* voice now. I tried to wrest control of it. Now that I knew that we possessed speech, having heard our first words, I was determined not to let it be used this way. I would tell our mother that we were fine and leave her be. But I could not find the voice, no matter how hard I concentrated.

I was mute. Binky was not.

He consumed her. Those tiny arms tightened, surprisingly strong and steady. I felt her breasts compacted against our ribs. I wanted to move our foot out from between her legs. But I had been subsumed. Binky, unburdened by my understanding of anatomy, did not waver or flinch. He had her and he would keep her as long as possible.

They all watched us as they passed on the way to the front doors of the school—parents, classmates, siblings and staff.

Stop being childish, I said. *Let her go.*

I was not heard. The glow inside our cave threatened to engulf us. We could bathe in it forever, close our eyes and never awake.

"That's enough!"

Her tone was sharp, frustrated. I could hear it, but Binky felt it. There was a moment of pure nothingness inside us, a void. Then the blade came slashing through the cave, long and sharp as a razor, just forged and nearly molten, blindingly yellow-orange-red. I ducked and it passed over me, singeing the ends of my hair and blistering the back of my neck. It was gone as soon as it came, but it left fissures in the walls, bloody red welts that healed instantly into scar tissue around me.

We were crying, again.

"Please, Binky," my mother said. "Please."

Somewhere a bell rang. I knew we would be late.

She returned our embrace and she whispered in our ear and slowly she made everything okay again.

FOUR

I DATED A second grade teacher for four and a half months. From the end of summer until Christmas. He was a big man and I could envision his students in awe before him. Hanging onto his every word, waiting for him to teach them. That's how I felt. I was twenty-seven at the time. With him, I finally understood that the ability to assert authority had nothing to do with spite or badgering. It is an aura of quiet competency that no one in my family ever had, despite our best efforts. He and I were supposed to go away for his winter break. I think we were going to drive up to Vermont. I suggested that I pick him up at school to get a jump on the traffic. Only after he declined did I realize he was closeted at work.

My own second grade teacher, Ms. Mittewag, terrified me. I remember this feeling of dread clearly, though I can't cite a single instance of punishment or ridicule. Just a general sense that my teacher was a tyrant.

I felt the panic rising as we approached my old classroom, passing rows of lockers that looked enormous. The fourth and fifth graders were like giants. Binky walked quickly, staying close to the wall. Finally, the classroom. The walls were lined with brightly colored admonishments—"wash your hands," "walk, don't run," "inside voices, please"—and displayed not a single implement of torture. No iron maidens, no stretching racks, no manacles.

Ms. Mittewag herself reinforced my confusion. As Binky took a seat near the back, I considered the petite woman at the front of the room. She was not the aged schoolmarm I expected. Just a young twenty-something with nervous eyes and a hopeful pout. True, there were wrinkles on her forehead that deepened as we filed into the room. Yes, as she surveyed us, a slight twitch started up in the corner of her left eye. She clutched the chalk a little too tightly and scraped it a little too hard on the blackboard as she wrote.

Hardly the stuff of nightmares.

And then she spoke.

"Open your books. Now!"

Ms. Mittewag was a screamer. This body of ours flinched, joining the others in snapping to attention. But I observed her at the front of the room and realized what I could not have known before. This woman was afraid of us. Barely out of school, probably teaching her first class, she was in over her head. I suspected that the first day of class she had started to yell and then couldn't get out of the pattern because the two dozen seven-year-olds had been conditioned to listen only to volume and grit.

"We'll start with times tables." No one moved. "First row. Twos and threes!"

The first row of students rose and started to drone through the times tables. One times two is two. Two times two is four. Three times two is …

Within minutes, the rest of us had retreated into our thoughts, leaving the wonders of multiplication behind. Binky and I ignored each other, like two people on an airplane acting as if they didn't share an armrest.

I tread lightly over what I thought I knew. This was my seven-year-old body, yet I still clung to my memories, my experience, my thoughts. My essence of who I was at age forty-two. It was all still there. I had not lost myself; I had been transplanted. But it didn't make sense. How could we both be here? That had to be a paradox.

Binky shifted in his seat, his thoughts somewhat akin to mine, failing utterly with his childish faculties to reason through the logic I myself was having trouble working out.

On the desk, he lined his pencils up, erasers forming a straight edge, the sharpened points aimed directly at Ms. Mittewag.

I set my sights on reading my young counterpart's thoughts. But he was no different than any other person around me—an impenetrable box, an unreadable mind.

There had to be a way for me to gain some control.

"Second row! Fours and Fives!"

We flinched again. Ms. Mittewag's voice, so sharp compared to the soothing drone of Binky's classmates. When all the students exhaled, the second row began.

One times four is four. Two times four is eight. Three times four is …

A deep silence fell over our shared space. Binky must have returned to his thoughts. The imbalance was starting to freak me out. I had to do something.

Binky's hands rested on the desk in front of me, the organizing of the pencils complete.

No. I forced myself to rethink that. Not Binky's hands. *My* hands. *Those are my hands*, I thought.

Focus. I can move that hand. It belongs to me.

I homed in on that hand—the skinny fingers, the hairless knuckles, the paper-thin nails. Ever so carefully, I scanned my mind for connections between the muscles in his wrists and the neurons in my brain. Assuming that I had a brain here, assuming that there was anything physical left of me …

No. That was irrelevant and again I swept my thoughts aside. The hand—only the hand.

Nothing happened. I narrowed my focus. The pointer finger. Just pick it up off the desk. A quiver, a twitch. Anything.

I strained, but felt about as much of a connection to that finger as I did to the pencil next to it. It was hopeless.

The hand moved. I was ecstatic. I must have been responsible. After all, I willed it to happen. It rose off the desk, slowly, like an object being levitated by a magician. I still felt nothing, which made me nervous. I tried to stop it, but I had no more control than before.

One finger popped out, like the saw on a Swiss Army knife, headed toward something on the lower part of Binky's face. When it entered his nostril and started to root around, I knew for certain that I had had nothing to do with the action.

Binky was picking his nose.

We were picking our nose.

Stop it, I said. *That's gross.*

You stop it. This is my hand.

I wanted to stop it. I wanted it all to stop.

Then, the question came. And like all difficult questions, it sounded quite simple when finally asked.

Who are you?

"Third row! Sixes and Sevens."

Ms. Mittewag distracted us momentarily, providing me with a pause within which to think, as Binky absorbed her tone, her words, taking time to worry about the inevitable ahead of him before processing that he was not in the spotlight yet.

I knew the answer to his question. More or less. At the same time I knew nothing.

One times six is six. Two times six is twelve. Three times six ...

It's complicated, I said.

I hear you. But no one else knows you're here. Are you 'in my head'?

He said that last phrase carefully, as if it were not his own. And I wondered who put it there. It sounded like something an adult had told him. I remembered seeing a psychiatrist after the rape. But the rape hadn't happened yet.

What is 'rape'? What hasn't happened?

I cleared my mind of those thoughts, shaking it like an Etch A Sketch, though I could feel the chill such actions put on our conversation.

I am you, I said. *I'm just a part of you. That's why no one else can hear me.*

Like in the cartoons.

I didn't understand, but Binky continued before I could seek clarification.

Sometimes the guy or the cat or something is about to do something and then there's like a little one of him on one shoulder and another little one of him on the other shoulder and one is white and one is red.

An angel and a devil, I said.

Yeah, maybe. One tells him good things and one tells him bad things. I think it was a cat. Or maybe Bugs Bunny.

You know that they are a part of him, I said. *Even though they're talking to him.*

Yeah, 'cause they look just like him. Just smaller. And different colors. And one of them has wings and the other one has horns. But you don't look like me.

That's true, I said.

Yeah, one is bad and one is good.

The angel is good and the devil is bad, I said.

Yeah.

The silence returned. The contemplative pause. Everything around me grew prickly, like a bath filled with warm water and needles.

Which one are you?

I was stumped. We are all both. Angel and devil. The inseparable dichotomy. Better to just say I'm the angel and be done with it. The moment had passed, however. Something had happened while I was thinking. Something in the classroom.

Binky sat stock still in his chair. I could feel the muscles tensed throughout his small frame, accentuating its dimensions and limits. Short breaths swirled around us like wind in a tunnel, trapped and impotent. I abandoned my thoughts and returned my attention to the classroom to discern the source of our disturbance.

Ms. Mittewag stared at us. And I felt what Binky felt—this woman hated us.

"Benedict! Are you LISTENING?"

She barked out the syllables of the last word, turning each into a threat.

We looked left and right. We sat in the fifth row and all the other kids on either side of us were standing. Looking at us. Smirking. Waiting for the ax to fall.

What happened to the fourth row? They were supposed to do eights and nines? They had finished. We had been distracted.

Ms. Mittewag motioned at the other children to sit. With a single slender, well-manicured finger—more suited to a princess than a witch—she beckoned us to our feet.

Binky stood.

I could feel the slight tremor in his jaw. Even if he knew the answer to the next question, his brain might be unable to retrieve it.

"Benedict! Tens and Elevens!"

I wrested myself away from Binky. This was no big deal. Who cares if a second-grade teacher with a Napoleon complex yells at you? It doesn't mean much in the general scheme of things. And what's easier than the tens in a times tables? *Come on, read my mind. Listen to me.*

But Binky was frozen. She might as well have slapped him. He tapped his tongue against the inside of his top teeth rhythmically and waited for salvation. Inside, there was a rush of sound—no thought, only emotion.

Binky, listen to me, I said. *Just repeat what I say.*

I strove with all my might to take control of the tongue, the voice box, the esophagus. I searched for them, and came up empty. My only option was to speak to Binky, not for him, so I yelled, trying to break through the white noise that surrounded us.

One times ten is ten, I started. *Two times ten is twenty.*

Binky spoke. Everything I said, he said. But I was not his voice. I did not speak.

We went faster. I could see Ms. Mittewag's features slacken in disappointment. Or was that amazement? As we powered through the tens and barreled into the elevens without slowing down, I hoped that I initially had read her wrong. Maybe she wasn't annoyed that we could clear her hurdle. Possibly she was happy that we had learned something.

That she had taught us something.

Eleven times eleven is one-hundred and twenty-one.

"Eleven times eleven is one-hundred and twenty-one."

Eleven times twelve is one-hundred and thirty-two.

"Eleven times twelve is one-hundred and thirty-two."

When we finished, there was silence in the room. Ms. Mittewag glared at us, but for the first time that morning there was a softness around her edges. Maybe even a hint of a smile in the corner of her mouth.

"Benedict. You may sit. Very good."

We sat.

For the rest of the morning we were left alone with our thoughts. Ms. Mittewag lectured on American History for a bit, some famous names and dates with no context. Then, she turned out the lights and showed us an episode of *The Electric Company*. Some kids fell asleep. Ms. Mittewag sat at her desk with a pile of papers, though she never turned a page or made a note.

Neither Binky nor I was willing to admit yet that we were stuck with each other. Or worse. That we needed each other.

Instead of allowing myself to think, I watched the screen, flooded with nostalgia, and marveled at how young Morgan Freeman had once been.

FIVE

Sitting there in the dark, from our seat in the back row, I could watch the entire room. Binky lost himself in the TV show, paying a hazy unfocused attention to the screen that allowed me freer rein. As my younger self became more distant, I clarified, zeroing in on details in his peripheral vision, asserting what I imagined to be my independence.

I didn't remember many of the kids in this classroom. Their faces and names eluded me. But I found that if I concentrated on someone and then gave Binky a nudge, just a quick poke, the name of the child would transfer to me. We were running a relay, passing the baton. All without ever diverting his attention from Spiderman on the TV using the word "contain" to tie up a bad guy.

Katrina Lopez sat in the front row. I remembered her. She was always quiet, but by high school she had turned into a beauty. Much sought after, never attained, since her father didn't let her date. Trina went off to Harvard after graduation and disappeared, as far as the rest of us were concerned.

I found myself breaking down the ethnic diversity of the class. When did I train myself to do that? Trina fell into the

"Hispanic" box. I didn't know that at the time; I didn't see her as anything other than a girl. Just as I didn't know that Helen Cho was Korean or that being Korean was different from Paul Miyazaki being Japanese. There was not a single black kid in the room and I felt embarrassed by that.

I fixed on a mousy little girl at the side of the room. Missy O'Neill. A tragic figure. All high schools have them. She "developed" first, sometime in sixth grade. It was a milestone for all of us. For me, it was the first time I noticed that boobs turned the guys around me into drooling idiots but had no visible effect on me. I was immune to tits. Missy thought she was ugly and no one told her otherwise. By sophomore year, she had slept with a handful of the guys, but she was convinced that Louis Kirk was the one who got her pregnant. He said it wasn't him.

I scanned the room and found Louis, leaning against the opposite wall, picking something out from under his fingernail. Two children, innocent, hardly capable of such acts. Yet, that is what they would become.

I continued around the room, identifying the other kids that stayed on with me in school and the ones who would move away and the ones who would transfer to private schools. All of us had our destinies laid out before us. But right here, watching *The Electric Company* in this darkened second-grade classroom, I knew that free will would elude them. All their decisions had been made, their fates decided. Missy would go off to have her baby and never return, those still being the days before teen mothers were media darlings, while Louis would escape any consequences, lettering in football and basketball and going to prom with Julie Dorchester, who had the good sense to use birth control. Katrina would go to Harvard. I would go to Columbia. Paul became a doctor. Helen smoked a lot of pot.

Some of us had productive lives ahead of us. Good jobs, healthy families, interesting hobbies. Some of us would die early. Some of us would never have kids.

Roger had wanted to adopt. He had all the brochures, had weighed the pros and cons of domestic versus international, toddler versus newborn. I let him do all the research—I made all the excuses.

We didn't have the money. We didn't have the time. Hadn't he seen how hard it was to raise a kid in the city? Who would want to bring a child into this troubled world anyway? I liked how our lives were right now, didn't he? Better not to mess with a good thing.

Ultimately I settled on a poisonous combination of self-hatred and social commentary. I don't want to subject a child to the discrimination of having gay parents. I beat that one into the ground. The argument struck a chord with Roger—after all, discrimination was built into the system. No country officially allows adoption by foreign gay couples. Even in New York City, it took some effort to find the right lawyer who knew how to game the system, who had the right contacts who would look the other way. At its core, adopting meant lying about who we were, and Roger did not lie. So Roger stopped talking about it for a while. But not for long.

I wondered what Binky regretted in his short life. I tried to remember anything I'd wanted to do differently at age seven and came up blank. In our shared space, our cave, the atmosphere gelled around us, encasing the moment in amber. We became sluggish together.

The note hit us in the shoulder. A perfect shot. It landed on our desk, a tightly folded triangle that I recognized as a paper football. Unmarked, its origin was undisclosed. Binky opened it easily, little fingers peeling apart the folds in practiced motions. There was a single word written inside, comprised of three clunky block letters.

FAG.

I could feel Binky sounding it out in his mind. In our mind. That word, so familiar to me, so many connotations, to him felt new and uncertain. He rolled it over his tongue and passed it into his ear. Of course, even at age seven, he knew it was an insult, but he did not know why.

Seeing it there, I could hear it issuing from hundreds of lips in hundreds of voices. From the frat boys and jocks throwing it casually in my direction at keg parties and bars—vindictive, vehement, a bit scared. From my college friends, playful and seductive, toying with the danger of it. In political discussions, repeated clinically until it lost any derogatory meaning in a vain attempt to take back the epithet and neuter it. Whispered by Roger in my ear—one of his misguided attempts at talking dirty.

We looked around the room for the author. I suspected that Binky knew who'd flicked it in our direction, but he wasn't talking.

The show ended. The lights went on. And then we were all lining up to leave the classroom.

Where are we going? I said.

Lunch.

There was a shiver in the word. I knew exactly why. Unsupervised activity, like lunch, could be perilous.

I EXPECTED CHAOS. My memory of the lunchroom was that they threw us all into this giant coliseum, locked the doors and let us tear each other apart. I could feel Binky's nervousness, which only increased my own disorientation. Whenever we moved from place to place, when Binky controlled us and the motions were unconscious—learned behavior, walking, sitting, reaching—I got an unsteady sensation, like being on a rocking boat in moderately rough seas. I was still not comfortable in my second chair position.

But as the lunchroom monitors ushered us to our seats and lined the walls, I realized that there was never a moment when we weren't being watched. Our classmates laid out their lunches, girls at one end of the table and boys at the other.

There were no riots, no hazing—just a hundred kids lined up and masticating like cattle.

The odors assaulted me. Tuna fish two seats down. A hardboiled egg kitty corner across the table. Chicken curry salad to my right. I could feel Binky swallow hard and try to breathe through his mouth as the smells attacked him. We fought off the nausea and took refuge in the contents of our own paper bag.

A cream cheese and jelly sandwich. A pickle. Cold turkey slices. A bag of crackers. Juice.

That was lunch? I wondered how he'd survived to become me. But Binky seemed satisfied, starting with the sandwich. It was only I who suffered, barely able to stomach the slimy coating of cream cheese on our tongue and the sweetness of the apricot jam that hurt our teeth. Luckily I was irrelevant in this matter. My thoughts did not affect Binky's enjoyment of the sandwich in the least. My psyche made only a stomach in some distant time churn.

Down the table, at the midway point where the gender shift occurred, one of the boys was mimicking *The Electric Company* announcer—"Heeeyyy, youuu guyyysssss"—which was making not only the boys but also the girls around him laugh. I could feel the boys at our end of the table hating him.

Binky crunched on the pickle. I wasn't sure I could take the combination, but he smiled at the salty-creamy-sweet concoction that swished around our mouth.

"You're a pussy."

The words were meant to provoke. We looked up to see Matt Ferguson shoving boys aside to sit across from us. He had been at the end of the table. Now he stared right at us. Binky glanced over at the lunchroom monitor, but she was nodding off standing up. I could feel him hunkering down, ready to absorb the blows.

Except that the kid was far from threatening. Where Binky

saw bulk, I saw pudge. Where he saw avarice, I saw ridiculous blather.

"What's for lunch, pussy?"

Binky stared at his pickle, frozen, about to bite. I strained to look at Matt through the veil of our eyelashes. He grinned, baring his teeth.

I remembered him. In high school, his size turned into obesity, not strength. They called him Fat Matt and he became sullen and lonely. Unlike me, able to hide my homosexuality behind an outer appearance of homogeneity, Matt was one of the unfortunate ones who could not mask his otherness. He might have had friends among the freaks and geeks, but he had spent years tormenting them and they had long memories.

Matt reached across the table and slapped the pickle out of our hand. We watched it fall to the floor. Even Binky understood that anything that touched that surface was lost forever. I felt the shudder within, the condensation starting to form on our windowpanes.

Don't cry, I said. *That'll be it.*

But the wave was forming, crashing toward us. Boys around us laughed, some nervously, others with malice, each one setting off a grenade and weakening our defenses. I could not let this happen. I was at that moment acutely aware that Binky was me and that I was about to make a fool of myself. That couldn't happen—not when the situation was so ridiculous, so easily ignored or diffused. I knew that a bully craved the reaction more than the action. I could deny him. I could starve him.

Fat Matt, I said. *That's what we called him in high school.*

The shivers subsided as Binky turned inward, curious.

High school?

Matt is going to be a huge tub of lard, I said. *No one will like him.*

Things started to get uncomfortably warm around me, like gears overheating from exertion. I realized that in my haste I had introduced a new concept. Knowledge of the future may be beyond the scope of what Binky could handle.

He is fat.

Yes, he is, I said.

Now we were looking—really looking—at Matt across the table. I could see it in the boy's eyes as he considered the change in our expression. The laughter fell away, replaced by anticipation. Things had become unpredictable and interesting.

"Aren't ya gonna eat that pickle, pussy?" Matt said.

He strived to regain his momentum, but there was a waver in his voice.

Pickle pussy. I repeated the alliteration in my head, enjoying the feel of it. Binky heard me and said it as well.

See, he's not worth crying over, I said. *He probably doesn't even know what 'pussy' means.*

What does it mean?

I'd walked right into that one. Roger used to accuse me of being unable to modulate my behavior to fit the age of my audience. We had that fight after dinner with the family of his college friend. I'd told a joke about a dildo in front of an eight-year-old. He told me I would never be fit to be a parent, and I responded that that wasn't news to either of us, and he fled the scene to go play pool at the bar down the street. That was early in our relationship, long before the photos of orphaned children began to appear on our coffee table.

But this wasn't just any child asking the question. I was asking myself and why shouldn't I provide the answer I already knew?

There was a rumble around me. The subconscious equivalent of clearing my throat. Binky waited patiently.

Pussy is slang for vagina, I said.

Silence. I thought that was about as straightforward as it could be.

What's a vagina?

It's a woman's private parts. Where you have a penis, women have a vagina. It's the ... hole ... you know, down there.

What had started out coherent dissolved into discomfort. But I resolved not to let myself fall prey to the obvious societal biases about discussing sexuality.

Oh.

"Hey, pussy!"

Matt snapped his fingers in front of my face. I looked at the other faces around the table. They were confused, maybe scared. I realized that we must have blanked out again, just as we had in the kitchen that morning. I wondered how often that happened, the complete retreat inside.

"You don't even know what that means," Binky said.

"Yeah, I do," Matt said.

The table waited. Matt's thick fingers balled into doughy fists.

"You're a pussy!"

We smiled and Matt flinched.

"A pussy is a vagina," Binky said. I recognized my voice within, the voice I would become. "Where boys have a penis, girls have a pussy. A ... hole."

Everyone stared at us now. Matt was forgotten. There was reverence in their eyes, a thirst to know what we knew.

Binky sensed his opportunity. He wanted to seize it, this unfamiliar attention. No one asked the inevitable question, the fear of being exposed as ignorant was too great. But everyone waited.

We needed an opening.

"You're still a fag," Matt said.

And everyone turned back to Binky for a definition.

A fag is a man who has sex with other men, I said.

Binky repeated my words. As I heard them issue from his mouth, in his high squeaky voice, I regretted that I was the snake giving these kids the apple. But it was too late to turn back now.

I started to explain to Binky and he started to explain to the kids around the table.

"Women have a hole so the man can put his penis into it. That's sex. That's how men and women make babies."

I could see in their faces that Binky was now to be respected. He had knowledge they only dreamed of. I could tell which of the boys had rummaged through their father's dirty magazines, which ones at least had a mental picture of the anatomy that didn't involve bathing with their sisters or watching their mothers get out of the shower.

I wanted to stop, but in so many ways, Roger was right. I could talk for hours about boundaries, but inherently I didn't understand them.

"When two men have sex, one man puts his penis in the butt of the other man."

We had gone too far. Matt slowly got up and moved back to his seat at the end of the table. No one ate. I wondered if the reaction would be the same with a group of seven-year-olds in my time, where millions of explicit images were available at the click of a mouse. Watching these kids' faces, I knew that at any age, there was innocence to be lost. I could feel it in the flush of our own face, as Binky processed what he had just said.

We all sat there, steeped in our own thoughts, waiting for lunch to end.

I remembered the night that I finally told Roger why I flinched sometimes when we were having sex. How sometimes, despite my attraction, my need, when I couldn't see his face, I would catch glimpses of those boys instead and that night and have to pull away to catch my breath.

"I'm not your sister's rapist," he said when I had finished. That was his only comment—angry and pointed, so unlike his usual psychoanalytic manner—before going to sleep.

The bell rang. Binky stood up and fell into line with the rest of the children. Queasy in motion, carried by his bird-like legs, I returned to class with him.

SIX

WE RETREATED TO our respective corners and rode out the rest of the day. The lunchroom conversation replayed in my head. *It will be all right*, I thought. There were only two more days left in this school year. All would be forgotten over the summer.

Ms. Mittewag told us to read to ourselves. We all sat at our desks in silence, books open. Ms. Mittewag stared at the clock, unwilling or unable to hide her desire to end the day, to conclude this year. I remembered my first year at the firm. That constant fear of not knowing what to do. I hadn't learned to fake competency. It seemed that every other lawyer knew that I was in over my head. I wondered if in those first few days of the school year, Ms. Mittewag had discerned those same doubts from the students in this class. How devastating for a new teacher to be exposed as a fraud by a roomful of seven-year-olds.

I looked for Binky, but he had sequestered himself completely. I had been here for less than a day, and there was much I didn't know about the architecture of this space we shared. I tried to see inside the cave, but the glaring brightness of the outside world made it impossible. Like staring into a glass house on a sunny day—nothing but your own reflection.

Two more days until summer. Are we going to camp? Do we take a family vacation? My memories failed me—I could not recall the coming summer.

Until I remembered. This was the summer after Sara's rape. That was why I wasn't finding the usual summer recollections of sunburns and sand and running and laughing and wearing shorts and playing games and counselors and campers and swimming in the lake and Capture the Flag and outdoor showers and fun. None of that would happen. Not this summer. This was the summer of psychiatrists and tears and anger and lawyers and cops and fear and unwanted media attention and silence.

The future stretched out before me, a long string of events that I had already experienced. Was I going to relive them all again? Was that my fate? Over the last few hours, things had occurred that I did not remember, events that I might or might not have lived through previously. Was that because *my* presence had changed things? Or had my intrusion into my younger self's head altered nothing?

I hoped that it was just my flawed memories that prevented me from divining what was to come, although then I would be doomed to repeat every mistake, every experience, every stumble as if I had never stumbled before. That could not be the purpose of this glitch in the universe, this unhappy accident that had cleaved me and sewn me back together so carelessly. This had to be more than an anomaly.

I was walking in circles, finding nothing.

I could feel our lungs working overtime in our chest, fluttering like a hummingbird's wings. Starting to hyperventilate. Panic. Short, clipped breaths humidifying the air before us. What I didn't know was if I had caused the physical reaction or if it was Binky, wherever he was.

Concentrate. Breathe. Distract.

Think of something else. Less troubling. Less existential.

I needed a task. But there was nothing I could do.

Names. Our names. Create a list.

Binky. That's what Mother called us as a baby. At some point, it stops being the family nickname. I don't remember when.

Benedict. The name on our birth certificate. An embarrassment. My mother had named my siblings Sara and Charles—nice, solid, uninteresting names. She had joked with my father that he could dub the next baby whatever he wanted. Neither of them expected to have three children. Then I came along—the accident—ten years after Sara. My father held my mother to her promise. He named me Benedict because I had betrayed them, extending their parental servitude by a decade. That's right—I'm Benedict Arnold. He thought it was funny; my mother did not.

Ben. What people have called me for most of my life.

Benny. An endearment reserved for close friends, lovers and other people who think they know me better than they really do.

Benji. What a girl on my freshman dorm hall called me for three weeks when she refused to believe I was gay and tried to seduce me. When I informed her that my name was Benedict, not Benjamin, she gave up on her quest, realizing that she did not actually know me at all.

Our breathing had returned to normal. Binky had not emerged. I realized that even as a passenger on this train I might be capable of derailing it, given the right circumstances.

The clock clicked the last few seconds of the day away, tapping them off deliberately like an exhausted woodpecker.

The bell rang. The children around us came to life, slamming books and shifting desks, heading for the door. Ms. Mittewag cracked a smile, possibly thinking of someone waiting for her at home with a glass of wine.

We were still, unmoving.

Come on, Binky, I said. *Time to go.*

He wasn't there. Ms. Mittewag watched us, frozen in our miniature desk, peering into a book, never turning a page.

"Benedict? Time to go home."

Her voice had changed. There was a different person inside her as well, someone who emerged into the light only at the end of the school day.

We still didn't move. I willed action. I screamed into the darkness and heard my words echo back at me. People had always told me that I was a thoughtful child, a dreamer, lost in my own world. Watching Ms. Mittewag approach us, I understood how the mysteries within me scared adults.

We were so still.

"Ben?" she said, kneeling in front of us. "Are you okay?"

Binky returned. He flowed through the walls around me, up through the floor, down from the ceiling, in pieces yet whole, and condensed before me. He came together and existed. I realized how limited I still was in my understanding, in my abilities.

We moved again.

Ms. Mittewag exhaled and we inhaled, relief filling the room around us.

"You did a good job today," she said, caressing us with her tone, encouraging us. I knew she would find her way, not in the next two days, but maybe next year. "On your times tables."

A glow surrounded us, a gentle fiery orange.

Without a word, just the hint of a smile, Binky piled up his books. We left the room.

Where did you go? I said.

Nowhere.

What were you thinking about?

I don't know. Nothing, I guess.

When I saw my father outside the school, standing by the car, the routine of those days returned to me. Memories triggered by stimuli. My mother dropped us off and went to work; my father picked us up.

My father had been a writer then. For one year, he stopped being a lawyer and started being a writer. It was one of the first times I understood that people could change. Later I learned that change did not always lead to success.

He spent hours in his office upstairs. Sometimes I would hear tapping behind that door, but often there was only silence. Sometimes muttered curses, like tiny puffs of steam from a boiling kettle.

When he finally left the old house on Sycamore and moved into an apartment, I helped him pack up the decades of detritus. I found a box marked "In Progress." He took one look at it and told me to put it out with the trash. But that night, while he slept, I read every word of his collected works. Twelve short stories and 227 pages of an unfinished novel. Most of it was dated 1976 and 1977, though some of the stories had been written earlier. After 1977, after June of that year, he stopped writing.

The prose was plain and a bit stilted. But the emotion was raw. Anger and sadness leached from those pages into the air around them, eating through the space between the words and the reader like battery acid. It was all science fiction, aliens, and space exploration, tinged with angst and ennui.

We got into the car and my father drove us the short few blocks to the high school in silence. As we pulled up to the curb, we saw Charles waiting. Three boys stood over him like a halo. They were speaking to him, but we couldn't hear with the windows rolled up and the air conditioning on. They had the smug expressions of unchecked bullies, relishing the effectiveness of their words. Charles stared stoically ahead. One of the kids pushed my brother and my father honked the horn. The bullies dispersed. Charles got into the front seat. My father pulled away into the slow-moving exodus of mid-size sedans without asking about the incident.

Between the two of them, the car filled up with a dark gooey discontent. I could feel it infiltrating our mind. Was this how parents infected their children? Could the moods transferred into those young bodies be as concrete as food and water?

The drive from the school did not take long.

Finally, my father spoke.

"Charles, I need you to watch Ben this afternoon."

"I've got D and D today."

My father turned his attention to my brother. All his cold, quiet wrath.

"I'm working. You watch Ben."

"He can watch himself."

"If you can't be bothered to participate in this family, you may not deserve that expensive toy we just bought you."

"It's not a toy. It's a computer."

But the argument was over. Charles had lost. He always did.

"You don't even work," Charles muttered under his breath.

I barely heard it. Binky's magical seven-year-old ears picked up the whispered syllables. My father heard it too. He whipped his head around, ready to drill full-bore into his son. But Charles must have looked scared or regretful or maybe just plain weak, because our father turned back to the task at hand, skidding to a stop in the driveway.

SEVEN

"**B**UT HE'S AN elf. Elves are graceful and sure-footed. They don't trip."

"You have a first-level elf. He tripped."

"I got to second-level last week."

"Fine," Charles said. "Second-level. You still tripped."

Eldon Vanderwaal glanced at his twin brother Archie, who just shrugged back. Like most twins, they were capable of speaking without words; unfortunately, they had lousy poker faces. Floyd Maple lay on the floor between them, glad not to be on the defensive. The three boys, each one of them two years younger than Charles and stuck in the purgatory of middle school, lay splayed across the floor, forming a semi-circle in front of my brother, who lorded over them from his position on his bed.

Charles was, after all, the all-powerful Dungeon Master.

"The dwarf should have tripped," Eldon said.

"What?" Floyd said, fondling his meticulously painted dwarf figurine. "I didn't trip."

"Dwarves are clumsier than elves," Archie said, supporting his brother. A familiar pattern.

"I have a twelve dexterity."

"The elf tripped," Charles said.

Binky was riveted by the discussion. Charles had told him to sit in the corner and he'd obeyed. He itched with the desire to play.

Charles laid his hand on the Dungeon Masters' Guide, like a politician being sworn in on a Bible. The three players fell silent.

"Would you like to roll for it?" Charles said.

A challenge. The gauntlet thrown. Eldon considered the consequences of his decision. Charles waited, grinning, ready to pounce.

During the ensuing long pause I surveyed the room. On Charles' desk was the beloved computer—an Apple II, with its clunky box monitor sitting atop the clunky box disk drive and the keyboard that couldn't decide if it was brown or gray. Charles had been one of the first kids to get a computer. He was always an early adopter. The first to have a computer or, later, an Atari or a Walkman. The first to see the new movie or read the new Piers Anthony. After making his millions, the first to buy the new car, private jet, vacation home.

Charles sought power where he could, and right now it was presented to him in the form of a 20-sided die, which he held out to Eldon.

"Fine," Eldon said. "I'll roll."

Charles dropped the die to the floor. Eldon grabbed it.

"One to ten—you trip. Eleven to eighteen—you don't trip." Charles paused and smiled. "Nineteen or twenty—you die."

Archie gasped. Floyd bit his tongue to stop from gloating. Eldon steeled himself for the most important role of his second-level elf's life.

Binky was intent on the outcome, rapt.

I remembered that feeling, that ability that children have to care deeply and unconditionally about something ridiculous, a knack that most adults have lost. Time stopped around us, all thoughts frozen and emotions idled.

"How can tripping kill me?"

A last ditch attempt at sanity.

"There is a spike in the wall. You will fall into it. Head first."

Acceptance from all present. Charles was the Dungeon Master, after all.

Eldon rolled.

"Six," Charles said. "You tripped."

But he didn't die. Relief all around.

"What did he trip over?" Floyd asked.

"It appears to be some sort of lever," Charles said.

"Oooh! I pull it."

"The elf is not strong enough. Only the human fighter can move it."

"That's me," Archie said. "I pull the lever."

Archie and Floyd waited. But Eldon, still angry at the indignity, shot back at Charles.

"I heard Keith talking about a party on Thursday."

"Yeah, down in the Grove," Archie chimed in. "A high school party."

Eldon twisted the knife. "You going?"

Charles stared him down.

"Of course I'm going," Charles said. "I'm in high school."

"You were invited?" Eldon said. His desire to wound had been replaced by genuine wonder.

"Keith said everyone's invited," Archie said.

"Not us," Floyd said.

There they were—Eldon, Archie and Floyd—doomed from the start. I searched my memories and could dredge up absolutely nothing about their future lives.

"Are we gonna play or what?" Charlie said.

And my brother. The kid who wanted with all his heart to believe he would go to a party he hadn't been invited to.

"Yeah, I pulled the lever," Archie said.

"The wall in front of you moves aside. You can tell there is a room beyond the opening. But there is something hanging in front of the passageway, blocking it completely. You cannot pass without touching it."

"I'm not touching it."

"Can we teleport through it?"

"Yeah, maybe if you were a blink dog."

Charles was looking at Binky. Binky glowed brightly at the attention. We grew warm, anticipating inclusion.

"You want to play, Binky?" he said.

I nearly lost my lunch as Binky nodded vigorously and scampered over to the other boys.

"A blink dog wanders into the room," Charles said, then to Binky. "That's you."

Binky barked like a dog, taking his role seriously. The boys laughed. I hated myself for being in on the joke.

Binky, I said, *don't get too excited.*

But he couldn't hear me. The light inside us drowned out my voice.

"What do I do?" Binky said.

Charles handed Binky the twenty-sided die.

"Roll," he said. "One to ten, you teleport through. Eleven to twenty, you run through."

Binky threw the die, too hard. It rolled under the bed.

"Idiot," Charles said.

Binky tensed up.

Please, I said. *Please don't care about this.*

Eldon fished the die out.

"Eight."

"The blink dog teleports through the portal. When he appears on the other side, nothing is blocking the entryway. But the mysterious hanging is now wrapped around the dog, devouring it with gastric juices. Within seconds, nothing is left of Binky the Blink Dog and the slime mold disappears through a crack in the floor."

What happened?

He killed us, I said.

"You killed me?" Binky said.

"Yeah, you can go back to your corner now."

Instead, Binky darted from the room, his cheeks hot and wet. I could hear the boys laughing behind us as we ran down the hall toward our father's office.

You didn't see that coming? I said.

No.

We sobbed.

You know he doesn't want to play with you, I said.

Shut up. Go away.

Don't bother dad, I said. *He's working.*

But we were already at the door. Binky sucked in his breath and held back his tears. The door was ajar. I saw the electric typewriter, switched on and abuzz, a piece of paper protruding from the top, half covered with words.

Our father was not sitting at his desk. Small noises came from the other side of the room.

Beep. Bong. Beep. Bong.

Rhythmic. Hypnotic.

Binky pushed the door open a bit farther. Our father sat near the window, in front of a small TV, a game controller in his hand, playing Pong.

Leave him be, I said.

Binky listened to me. We retreated to our room.

EIGHT

MY MOTHER STOOD behind us, her discontent thickening the air. She slopped a ladle of macaroni and cheese on our plate, tapping the spoon twice before moving on to my brother. For about an hour, I had been preoccupied by a gnawing pain. Sitting at the dining room table, with a full plate in front of Binky, I realized that we were starving, having not eaten much at lunch. Binky shoveled food into his mouth, using his spoon and his fingers. The wet, slapping sound of teeth chewing noodles was only interrupted by the occasional pile drivers of crunching carrots and cucumbers. When she finished serving Charles, my mother put the casserole dish down next to my father. She took her seat at the other end of the table and kept her eyes on him as she started to eat.

Binky refused to look at Charles, which was complicated by the fact that he sat directly across from us. Charles tried to catch Binky's eye. He knew that something had stopped his younger brother from ratting him out, and he relished the power of that, whatever the cause. But Binky was steadfast, resting his eyes on the silverware, the napkins, his lap, our mother's face. Now, food became the only thing in his world.

He devoured it with evangelical zeal, leaving me free to think of other things.

Peripherally, I watched our mother watch our father. She was waiting for something. He knew it, employing many of the same avoidance techniques as his youngest son.

The last time I saw my mother was the day she drove me into the city, delivering me to college. Columbia was only a couple hours away from our home in Connecticut, so I had not brought all of my things. I could always take the train home to get what I had left behind. Double-parked outside the dorm beside all the other families, we carried my suitcases and duffle bags and stereo inside. She met my roommate and chatted with his parents. It all seemed normal. Until it was time for her to leave. She grasped me tightly and cried. My embarrassment stretched the length of the block. This was New York City—in that single minute that she held me, a million people could have witnessed my shame, from the hundreds of windows facing us, from the countless cars driving by, from the open doors of the other dorm rooms in the hallway.

Only later would I wish I could return to that moment. I dreamed of pulling her closer, rather than pushing her away.

Tears streaming down her face, my mother kissed me on the cheek, got into the car and drove away from me forever.

I was eighteen. I was an adult in my own mind and apparently in hers. She had fulfilled her maternal duties, staying with my father—a man she no longer loved—until I went away to college, dwelling in a house tainted by the thick smear of tragedy. Logically, any observer would expect me to do as my brother had done. Once Charles was liberated from the nest, he never returned. He made it clear that he didn't need any of us. So maybe my mother believed that I would do the same, never feeling her absence.

She was wrong.

Fatigue weighed on us all as we ate in silence. My mother had put in a long day managing the bookstore, spending all day on her feet. My father was exhausted from not writing. I could see the strain on their faces, in the way they lifted the leaden forks to their mouths. Charles was also worn out, but in a more satisfying way, like the high after a marathon. It had been a rough and tumble game of D&D with his friends—lots of arguing and reveling. Binky, listening intently through the wall he shared with Charles, had suffered.

Binky and I were also bone-tired from navigating our entwined existence. It had been only ten hours.

No one knew if Sara was tired or hungry or alone or alive. Her absence was deeply felt, there being a full, untouched place-setting laid out before her chair.

I had listened to my mother make all the obligatory pre-dinner phone calls to Sara's friends, or at least the friends she used to have in the long-ago time when she last confided in my parents. With each call, each act of contrition, my mother wilted. I sensed that this was a common ritual—the search for Sara. There was not much effort invested in it, no real hope for success. My mother gained some minor comfort from the words spoken to her by the parent on the other end of the line, though the effect was temporary. The final phone call made, she went to the kitchen to finish making dinner, defeated.

There were no cell phones in 1977. We were all disconnected. Sara could hide in plain sight.

Binky asked for a second helping and continued his gluttony. Finally, my mother spoke to my father.

"Did you call the doctor today?"

"Doctor?" my father said, his mouth half-full.

"You know, for …"

She pointed at Binky, off-handedly, like shooing a fly.

"Oh," he said, using a piece of lettuce as a scoop for the salad dressing. "No. I'll call tomorrow."

Now he did look at her and she did not blink. Binky realized that something was happening, possibly because he had eaten enough to quell the rumbling ache inside of him. He looked up at Charles, forgetting the day's events long enough to seek assurance. He found none. Our brother, fork dangling from his fingertips, was bracing for the fight.

"I asked you—"

"I didn't have time," he said. "I was working."

She had no response to that. Not yet anyway. Maybe in another few months, if there was still no progress, no product to show, no heavy stack of paper to hold in her hands. But for now, my mother had to resign herself to the fate of the artist's wife. The process was mysterious, unfathomable to her, and therefore she had no choice but to accept his words at face value, as a literal representation of the situation at hand.

The ontological truth: He was working.

She suspected that he was abusing her ignorance, but could not prove it.

"Fine," she said.

Her only remaining move, to get up and clear the table, was executed with a chill that left icicles hanging from the eaves of our house. A blizzard in June.

"Finish your vegetables," our father said, then, "Go do your homework."

Charles and I obeyed, finishing our iceberg lettuce, uninterested in correcting him by pointing out that with only a couple of days left in the school year, there was no homework to be done.

WE HAD BEEN in bed for about an hour when Binky pulled back the covers and tiptoed toward the door. Our mother and our father had taken turns tucking us in and reading us stories, never touching each other as they performed the changing of the guard. For so long I had assumed—aided by memory—that all our problems began on that night when Sara was raped. But the truth was that my family began to dissolve long before that. Charles was already angry. Binky had problems—festering, brewing, unformed and juvenile—but definitely present. Our family was a sugar cube, porous and never designed to remain solid, slowly disintegrating in a humid room. The rape was merely a dousing that sped up the process. Sara was already planning her escape. She was already gone.

Confident that everyone had retreated to their evening activities, each family member engaged in solitary pursuits, tapping on their typewriters and computers, reading novels and magazines. Binky poked his head out into the quiet hallway then snuck across the hall into Sara's room to await his sister's return. Binky anticipated my question.

I do this every night.

She doesn't mind? I said.

She wants me to.

A craving shook us. It belonged to us both. We both needed, more than anything, the contact with Sara. This was a common desire, a mutual goal.

I had missed her for so long.

Why do you miss Sara?

I did not know what to tell Binky. How to explain. He still did not understand, though I suspected he would, soon enough. I thought I had hidden my thoughts from him. Surely he hadn't heard me at dinner when all I could think about was how much I hated and resented our parents.

But what if he had? Would that be so bad? I worried that I was becoming subsumed. Mostly I wondered if that was what I wanted. How easy it would be to give in to Binky. To lose the burden of age and knowledge into youth and innocence. To disappear. Maybe that was why this transfer had happened, because I was meant to suffer the blows as a child again and again and again, a never ending loop in time, trapped between seven and forty-two for all eternity.

I heard Binky whimpering. Like a dog cowering after a blow. A broken animal.

I don't understand.

I'm sorry, I said. *I don't want to scare you.*

But you do scare me.

How? Tell me and I'll stop.

Why are you here?

Again, the unanswerable question.

Tell me.

Outside, a car engine, proudly altered and abused, the same vehicle that had taken her away that morning. Binky forgot me completely, even as he drew me to the window to look for Sara. There was movement within the car. I assumed that she was making out with X, saying good-bye, but Binky just waited without judgment until finally Sara emerged, radiant, into the night.

Sara, I said. *That's why I'm here. For Sara.*

The wait for Sara was interminable. Binky sat on her bed, ensconced among her stuffed animals, remnants of her lost childhood. We heard the yelling downstairs—my mother, my father, Sara—and we waited. Binky and I were silent.

Then, she arrived. Binky nestled deeper into the fluffiness of the bears and dogs and cows at the foot of her bed. Sara strode into the room. The argument with our parents seemed barely to have touched her. Such was her confidence, her joy, her satisfaction with herself and her life. Sara commanded the room. We were beholden to her.

Binky, squirming at the edge of the bed, could not contain his happiness. It was difficult, but I separated again from him, realizing for the first time how wound up he had been all day, how wracked and consumed by doubt and care. Everything had been a struggle, a constant internal conversation about right and wrong with no apparent resolution. Nothing had felt right. Until now.

Be quiet. She doesn't know I'm here. I always surprise her.

In our cave, that anticipation crackled like ball lightning streaking above us.

Sara played her part. She hummed and walked past us,

eliciting a shivery giggle among the stuffed animals. Sara did a twirl in front of us, performing.

"I do hope that Binky got to bed okay," she said, every word a smile. "I'm sooooo sorry I didn't get to sing a lullaby."

We exploded, a blast so intense that I doubled over in pain as Binky leapt to his feet.

"I'm right here!"

Sara squealed in mock delight, and we did a little dance on the bed, pounding our feet into the bouncy mattress. I fought against the nausea and focused on my sister's blue-gray eyes.

"You scared me," she said, lifting a finger to her lips. "Shhhh. We don't want mom and dad to know."

"It's our secret," Binky said.

"Yes, our secret."

When Sara hugged us, all the nausea and pain went away. All the warmth and light disappeared for a moment as well. Binky closed his eyes. For a split second, I was back in the cave, alone.

"How's my favorite little man today?"

Her words rang throughout the cavern like a bell. Binky opened his eyes again. The quick transition from one world to the next set me reeling.

"Good."

When Sara let go of us, the loss was devastating.

Binky rejoined the animals, settling in for the next phase of their nightly ritual.

Sara walked over to her dresser. We watched every move. She flipped through a stack of records, LPs. Those anachronistic vinyl disks that she left behind when she went to college. Those records that I took from her room after she killed herself, before my parents had a chance to throw them away. The LPs that still live with me, in my New York apartment, wherever, whenever I return.

She plucked out *Rumors*. Fleetwood Mac. Spinning the

WE   59

cardboard sleeve around in her hand like an illusionist about
to dazzle an audience.

"Best. Album. Ever."

The black circle slid out into her waiting hand. She placed it
on her record player, moved the needle to the track she wanted
to hear.

Binky tapped his little foot on the mattress as the familiar
opening to "Don't Stop" issued from the tinny speakers on the
turntable. A golden oldie to me—top forty to her.

Telling me never to stop thinking about the future.

My consciousness was flooded with the memory of Bill and
Hillary dancing at the 1992 Convention. I was watching on TV
with friends and we all started dancing and we truly believed
in them. I had done some canvassing, some phone trees—we
all did—talking to other gay men from a DNC generated list
and we all agreed with each other and had already made up
our minds and it was just a big party.

But there was no Clinton. Not yet. It took me a moment
to summon the name of Carter, the current White House
resident. There had been no Reagan, no Bush I, no Clinton,
no Bush II, no Obama, not yet. So much history to come—the
hostage crisis, Iran-Contra, the first Gulf war, 9/11, my fall.

Sara danced back into my consciousness, though Binky had
never stopped tracking her. She had shed her clothes, stripping
down to a bra and panties. To her there was only the song, a
perfect pop nugget that had no context beyond its unbearable
catchiness, and the night ahead of her.

Clothing flew out of her closet and drawers. Binky laughed
as it rained down on us. A shirt fluttered down to the bed. A
pair of pants hit us in the face.

"Sorry, Bink," Sara said. "You okay?"

I felt us nod.

Sara was asking us questions. This shirt or that one, these
pants or those shorts, which shoes. I zoned out, back into my
own self. Fashion had never interested me at any level. A gay

man comfortable in flannel and corduroy, I was a subject of curiosity. An endearing quality as far as Roger was concerned. Never hip. Never fabulous.

I looked up, along with Binky, and saw that Sara was dressed now. Wearing a flowery, floppy, tie-dyed top with too-tight hot pants and white fringed boots. The latest in teenage hippie disco chic. The amalgamation made me laugh. I couldn't help it. But Binky wasn't interested in my opinion.

Shut up!

I realized that my reverie, my musings about future events and our family, had allowed him to be alone with Sara. He was not happy to have me interfere again.

So I grew quiet and simply observed.

"I've decided," Sara said, her voice dropping to a gentle whisper.

She climbed onto the bed with us, crossing her legs. Binky took his cue and lay on his back, resting his head in her lap. We looked up at her, letting just a few strands of her long blonde hair tickle our face.

"X is the one," she said. "Thursday I'm going to let him. After the party."

Sara licked her lips. I peered into her hopeful face, upside down above us, and saw her need for approval, a chink in the façade that hadn't been apparent before.

"Last day of school. A new beginning."

We smiled and the room smiled and she smiled and she leaned forward and drowned us in her garden shirt and young breasts.

That's a good thing, right?

I didn't know what Binky was asking me.

Finding "the one"—that's a good thing. She's happy.

It can be good, I said. *But it's complicated.*

Why?

Adults don't always know what they've found, I said.

Is Sara an adult?

Not exactly, I said. *And that makes knowing harder.*

You're confusing me again.

I'm sorry.

There was a long pause. I felt things growing sluggish around me. Binky's thoughts grew further apart and settled to the floor like flower petals at our feet. Sara absentmindedly ran soft fingers through his hair.

Binky was falling asleep.

Sara eased our head off her lap, putting a pillow underneath it. Our eyes popped back open. She kissed our cheek and walked away.

Is this about the stuff you told me about before? Sex?

Yes, I said.

Is Sara going to be okay?

I forced my mind to go blank. I drove all thoughts away. I told Binky what he wanted to hear. What I needed him to hear at that moment.

Yes, I said.

The lights went out. As Binky's eyelids drooped, we watched Sara open her window slowly and exit onto the roof. Behind our darkness, after the world went completely black, I alone heard the window drop down to the sill. I alone heard Sara slip away into the night.

This was my chance. I could feel it. As the world we shared grew quiet and still, I thought this might be the end of my dream, my vision, my hallucination. It could still be that none of this was real. The calm descending on us now could be the prelude to my return to the hospital room, where I could forget that I had seen Sara again, where I could forget that she had once been full of life and hope.

I still believed that I could free myself of the burden before me. As Binky drifted irretrievably away, things around me started to come into focus.

NINE

I WAS BACK in the cave. While Binky slept, the entire world, my new world, quieted down. There had been a constant thrum and whoosh of that young mind all day, working and expanding, growing and struggling. Most of that disappeared, leaving only a low rumble, the faintest hint of far-off machinery running through the night. I sat alone in this cave, with its rounded eroded surfaces wet and organic to the touch. The walls of the chamber glowed, as if covered with a bioluminescent moss.

I was tired, but I could not sleep. My eyes would not close. I tried to blink and discovered I could not shut out the world even for a moment. Craving self-imposed darkness, I demanded that my eyelids fall, clamping shut against the world beyond. But the cave would not disappear. Now, the panic surged. I had no eyes of my own. No ears, no tongue, no nerve endings. I was incorporeal—without body, without weight. But I existed. Independent of Binky, even as I was dependent on him. A hitchhiker, a parasite. I was not sure if I could live without him. I looked at my hands. They existed. I clapped them together, making a satisfying echo. I cleared my throat and relished the sound emitted from within me.

I am here, I thought.

Yet still I could not blink. No respite.

I needed to touch my eyes, feel the lids that enveloped them, tickle my finger with the delicate lashes. My hands neared my face—where my face should have been—but then they were lost. I could sense that they were there, fumbling around in the vicinity of where my eyes should be, but I saw nothing except the cave around me. My invisible fingers probed for familiar features—eyes, a nose, ears, lips—but they found nothing. Instead, they started to numb, as if I had plunged them into a bucket of ice water.

I pulled my hands out of the void, holding them away from me as far as I could reach. They came into focus again. Two hands. Ten fingers, which I wiggled manically just to be certain. I felt my throat closing up, drying out from the hyperventilation. I doubted that even that sensation was real, which only served to hasten the progression of it. Total panic. I thought I might pass out, but grew even more frantic when I wasn't sure that I could. What if I just spiraled with dread forever without even the possibility of falling unconscious? The migraine was centered in my temples, a pain that I could usually massage away with my fingertips. But my head had become a phantom limb, never to be touched.

No. I needed to stop this. I needed a task. *Focus. Distract.*

But there was nothing to do here.

I thought about Roger. What would he think of all this? He would have professional interest in the adult being subsumed by the psyche of the child. Not to mention the personal fascination with both sides of that equation being me.

When we first started dating, in that tentative period when you are willing to be enthralled by anything your new paramour has to say, we told each other stories about work. I would regale Roger with tales of document searches through thousands of boxes and how I marshaled dozens of interns and paralegals to find the nuggets that would catch witnesses off guard during depositions. With him hanging on my every word, my rationale for when to use a blue highlighter or when to choose orange instead seemed to be of monumental import.

For his part, Roger walked me through the history of psychology. This was partly because I made it very clear that I wasn't interested in hearing funny stories about his actual work as a therapist. I had been to so many psychiatrists in my life that it stressed me out to think that even the good ones got distracted or, worse yet, made fun of their patients, giving them silly pseudonyms to maintain a veil of anonymity. So instead, he told me about historical theories and tried to explain brain architecture. He once drew me a map of the brain with all its nooks and crannies, carefully labeling the lobes. But I must have come up with a blank stare because I remember him simplifying to describe the brain as a series of rooms, each with a single function. The doorways between the rooms allowed for the communication between systems. I knew he was dumbing it down for me, but I didn't mind. I was falling in love.

The conversations I remember best concerned Freud. Roger thought it was all a load of crap. The lust for one's mother and hatred of one's father. The hysteria driven by sexuality. The interplay of anthropomorphized personality traits. But the subject of Freud and his theories was also the most interesting. Freud seemed more like fiction than science to me. I loved Roger's description of the id as the unchecked monster in your mind. The superego as the manifestation of your morality, the sum of what you'd learned about right and wrong. The two twinned aspects of your personality working together to help you survive, even though they should inherently be in conflict. Roger once described the ego as the small child who will always be stuck in the middle between what it wants and what it thinks it should do.

That was Binky. Asking if I was the angel or the devil. The id or the superego. I didn't know the answer. Because I wasn't just a part of him. He was part of me.

The pain tore through my head. This train of thought wasn't working. I pinched the back of my hand. I felt that pain, but it did nothing to diminish the throbbing in my head. It was real. I was real. Of course I had a face. I envisioned my features, rebuilding them one by one. But they all came out wrong. It was someone else.

There had to be something else. Something outside me. A task.

I cast about and found a passageway at each end of the cave where before there had appeared to be only solid walls. My task was clear. I had to explore. The pain began to recede, if only slightly. I considered the two possible paths.

In one direction, the hum of machinery was perceptibly louder, issuing from a distance down the passageway. That was the direction I needed to go. I ran toward it, feeling that familiar urgency, the need to complete my task as quickly as possible. The passageway was barren and dark and dry. The floor had no give under my feet. In my haste, I lost my balance and scraped the wall with an outstretched hand. Flecks of dried matter fluttered to the ground. It was not long before the tunnel grew smaller and smaller until it was merely a crawlspace. That was where I finally stopped my sprint. In between gasps, I heard the machinery ahead. I got down on my stomach and peered into the crawlspace. Claustrophobia gripped me. It looked too small to pass through, even though I could tell that it opened into a larger chamber just a few feet away. I inched forward into the small opening. I could feel the walls on all sides of me. They were pliable, not rigid. These walls undulated and breathed. They pushed against me, constricting like a python. I started to panic again, resisting the urge to push back into the arid tunnel, back to the safe chamber where I had started out.

Then, I was through the tunnel, into the next room. I looked back. There was only an open doorway leading back to the cave. The shrinking tunnel had been nothing more than an illusion.

This room was about the size of an affordable studio apartment in Manhattan. I could stand up without bumping my head on the ceiling. I could walk in a reasonably sized circle without running into a wall. Thousands of tiny slits, like paper cuts with rounded edges, covered the walls. I touched one and it shrunk away from my fingers, wet and soft to the touch. The urge to pry it open and see what lay beyond was great, though ultimately fear prevented me. On the other side of the room, through a simple arched opening, I could see another chamber. But my view was obstructed. A shimmering curtain hung in the doorway. It glistened with life, slickly covered in fluids. The thing appeared to breathe. It resembled what I had thought of when Charles described the slime mold in the Dungeons and Dragons game.

This was my task. I had to explore on.

One to ten, I trip, I thought. *Ten to eighteen, I don't. Nineteen or twenty, I die.*

I leapt forward, through the thin layer of muck between the two rooms. As I thought might happen, it did not contain me. Now, in the new room, I looked back to see another wide open gateway. There were no slime molds, no gastric juices to devour me.

In this room, the walls were covered with countless tiny puckered pores, wide enough to poke a toothpick into. Roger might have called them glory holes for sprites, but he was like that, managing at times to be crude and bizarre and not particularly funny in a single statement. These walls sighed. A gentle rush and retreat of whispering breeze surrounded me, but I felt nothing on my skin.

The hum of machinery still lay beyond. Possibly below.

The panic had evaporated, leaving only reckless abandon in its wake.

At the far end of this room was a hole in the ground, a fireman's pole extending down. I remembered being fascinated with firemen as a child, though I could not recall why. The heroism, maybe. Possibly the understanding that society valued these men. Or it could have just been the cool trucks. As an adult, of course, I understood exactly why I loved firefighters—those shirtless calendars, the strength of those muscular bodies emerging from the fire coated with a layer of ash and bathed in the cologne of imminent death.

I slid down the pole, into a different world.

Colder. Darker. Harder. Rocks of various sizes covered the floor, shifting beneath my feet. I needed to take care with my footing. The fireman's pole, so smooth and metallic in the chamber above, was a thick column of rock down here. All around me, stalactites and stalagmites jutted from the ceiling and floor. Dust filled the air, thick enough that I felt the need to sweep my hands before me as if clearing spider webs. I was seized by the notion that the dust wanted to cover me, to drift into me, to tell me things.

Then the world lurched out from under me. The entire chamber spun, like a gyroscope, and I was floating in the middle of it. The queasy feeling returned. Binky had been sleeping deeply in one position, and I now realized he must be shifting, moving out of deep R.E.M. This room continued to spin as I hung there, waiting for stability to return. I saw stalagmites and stalactites reach for each other, twist around and grasp like tentacles, then retreat. I fell back into the shifting stones on the floor as the chamber righted itself and went silent once again.

As I traveled farther from the original chamber, the world seemed to become less coherent, each space more concerned with its purpose than with explaining itself to me. Only in that first room had I been completely comfortable, had my bearings, at least until the onset of the headache. That was where I belonged.

I looked up at the hole in the ceiling. There were clear

handholds in the rocks near it. I could easily scale that wall and leave. At the other end of the room, there was another passageway, a gentle decline into a place where I could clearly hear the machinery. The panic returned at the thought of going back, my task incomplete. There was farther to go, even if each new room felt more like a trap. I did not have a choice. I never do.

The path to the next room was not a passageway, but a slide. The chute, lined with mucous, was uninviting. At the end of it, more darkness awaited. A stench rose from within. A pounding. A rasp. The place below, down the slide, reeked of primordial ooze, of beginnings and uncertainty, of frailty and fervor.

I jumped, feet first, into the abyss.

The slide was as slick as it looked and, about halfway down, I decided that taking it had been a bad idea. It didn't help when I landed on my ass in a foot and a half of muck, somewhere down below. I was at the bottom of a well, looking up into a black void that stretched on endlessly over my head. The terminus of the chute was also above me, just beyond my reach. I had found the source of the mechanical noise. The gurgling and hissing and thumping and groaning surrounded me. The water at my ankles was alive with vibrations and motion. There was no other way out. I had indeed found the end. I touched the wall and the well shivered around me. It felt like putty. I dug my fingers in to create a handhold, thinking I could climb back to the chute.

We stopped breathing.

I could feel it, only for a terrifying moment. Our throat constricted. Our lungs went fallow. We forgot how to take in air.

Then, the well convulsed. I was tossed away, falling back into the muck. The indentation I had made stayed intact. I had done damage. I could feel it. Around me and inside me. Inside us. A change in the balance. *I shouldn't be here, not in this primitive elemental place*, I thought. Again I looked up the tube, which curved slightly away from me far in the distance. Suddenly the entirety of it hit me—that shape, familiar from Roger's drawing on the cocktail napkin. I was in the brain stem. Not *the* brain stem. *My* brain stem. The center of all my automatic responses. I had a particularly vivid memory of Roger talking me through that part of the brain because as he had touched my lips, my chest, my stomach as he described the unconscious functions controlled by the stem. Digestion, circulation, respiration. I wanted him to keep going lower. This was where it happened, deep in this well. Normally off the beaten path. This was a place where no one should be allowed to interfere. Damage here could kill me.

When Binky's eyes were open, I lived with him in the outside world. But when he closed his eyes, when he shut me off from the stimuli, I lived literally inside his brain, our brain. There was real solidity here, I was sure—tissue and neural connections, the anatomical stuff of consciousness. And yet, Binky and I both needed to layer a structure on top of that, a façade that roughly simulated what was outside of us. For me, it was a series of rooms—all that I could comprehend. I was probably nothing more than a blip of an electrical impulse firing along a synapse, but I couldn't see it that way. I could only experience what I could visualize, limited by my high school biology, a freshman entry-level psych course and whatever pieces Roger filled in. I wondered how much more he would have visualized in this world. I was disappointed in myself on his behalf.

The indentation in the wall, made by my hand, had not filled in.

I needed to get out. My mere presence could doom us, today and tomorrow. How stupid I was to think I could wander around without consequences. The handhold I made in the wall mocked me, like a scar from a failed suicide attempt. What if that dent I had created became a lesion decades down the road that led to a cancer I had not yet contracted? What if it was my own fingerprints that would eventually seal my fate?

My throat closed up tight.

But there is no need for air, I told myself. *You do not need to breathe.*

My hands started to tingle.

But those are not real. Those fingers, those wrists, those palms—nothing but a manifestation, a delusion.

My tongue swelled, my heart cramped, my head ached, my kidneys imploded, my spleen burst, my toes curled, my eyes burned, my stomach swelled, my muscles twisted, my ligaments tore, my bones broke.

I felt all that I wasn't. And all that I was.

I thought I had fallen, but it was the watery muck, the bile, that had risen to lap at my waist.

I tried to breathe. I tried to think.

I had failed. Again.

I had to fix it. I lunged for the dent I had made. I could smooth it back over, replace the divot. I could make it perfect again.

But something took my feet out from under me, dunking me into the bile.

Everything that I had ever done, wrong. Everything that had ever been, wrong. Had I set all of that into motion all myself? My self. Then, in childhood, and now. Me and him. Us.

Were we responsible for all future events, unwittingly and as one?

Or was it just me? Not Binky. Just *me*.

I was floating. It was not water surrounding me, but our very being. I knew that now. This place wanted to be rid of me. I stopped wanting to breathe. I bobbed upward, my feet leaving the floor of the well. The liquid carried me. Soon, I was at eye-level with the hole I had made in the wall. Already it was healing, hardening. Then it was gone, hidden under the seething liquid.

I let go, and all physical sensation ceased. I caressed this nothingness, the complete lack of connection to a body. *This is how I will die*, I thought. *In peace.*

But that was not to be. The bile that carried me upward diverted into the slide. It was pushing me out, all the way up that slimy chute, effortlessly, until it spit me back into the previous room.

Panic subsided, replaced by pain. It amazed me how real the sensations experienced by this avatar, this false body that I inhabited, felt. The stones on the floor of this room dug into my neck, my back, my calves. I had fallen between two stalagmites. Upon closer observation, they seemed to be made of flesh, not rock. Solid, calcified, but organic. I did not think. I reached out and grabbed a pillar in each hand. I yanked them toward each other, trying to pull myself to my feet. The world spun out from under us again. The room came to life. All the columns started to wave frenetically about, searching for contact with the others, shivering alone, unchecked. We lost control of our small body completely.

Again I was expelled. This time the stalagmites tossed me up to the stalactites which spit me out past the fireman's pole into the next room. The world continued to rumble and shake, a seven on the Richter scale. I did not even try to find my feet this time, instead crawling to the center of the room. Here, the puckered mouths on the wall had widened, each one frozen in a silent scream, each now large enough to crawl through.

"Binky!"

The word blared from every mouth on the wall, each one louder than the rest, a thousand pitched screams blending with a thousand unbearable explosions. My body shattered into pieces that scattered around the room, then oozed back together, only to be demolished again.

"Binky! Can you hear me?"

Within the volume, underneath the pain, I recognized the voice of my sister.

I stumbled into the next room, bit by bit. The tremors

lessened to aftershocks. I caught the breath I didn't need. The breath I craved. Here there was still darkness. The room with the paper-cut slits covering the walls. Here I was safe. But only for a moment.

"Binky, please," Sara said. "Wake up."

"Sara, what's going on?"

It was my mother. The voices came from the room next to where I currently sat, the cave where I had started out and the only place—I now knew—where I had been truly safe.

"Binky? What happened?"

I felt us being moved, probably carried back to our room.

"Why was your brother on the floor of your room? What is going on here?"

"Charlotte, calm down." My father was there too.

"I will not calm down."

"He was shaking." Sara again. "His whole body."

"He's not shaking now," my father said.

"It stopped."

"Sara, are you stoned?"

"Binky, can you hear me?" Sara said.

"The boy's sleeping," my father said.

"Why was he in your room?" My mother, an accusation.

"He was fine when I left," Sara said, clearly shaken.

"When you left?" My mother was asking the questions. I imagined my father retreating. "Sara, where did you go?"

"You don't care about us. Binky was having some sort of seizure. And you don't care!"

The slits on the walls started to flutter. They were widening. Slowly. I watched them and dreaded what I knew was coming.

Binky opened his eyes.

My world was destroyed again. The light burned through me as the paper cuts rounded into a million eyes. I was blinded by what Binky saw. Each ray of light ate through my flesh. The brightness consumed me. The voices got louder, but I could not hear them anymore.

Then, I was myself again. Somehow, I had scrambled back into the cave where I had started. The place where everything was in proper perspective—voices, visions, movement, all neatly packaged and understood by my consciousness. The place where Binky knew I would be safe. Back in the relative haven of this mostly barren cave, I believed that maybe my younger self had placed me here on purpose. To protect me.

Our eyes were open. We were being carried into our bedroom. We looked up into the face of our father. I could feel that this anxiously sought-after contact occurred rarely. My distant father. The man who was untouchable. I had always attributed that to his reaction to the rape of his daughter. I had been naïve. We were still tired. Still mostly asleep. Strong arms lowered us into our bed. Then he was gone and our mother's hand raised the covers up around our shoulders and brushed our cheek.

"Goodnight, Binky," she whispered. "I love you."

Time passed. A minute, maybe less. A hushed conversation continued between my mother and sister.

"I know what I saw. He was shaking."

"Of course he was. He fell off your bed. Where you left him. When you went out and got stoned."

We turned our head to look at Sara and our mother, silhouetted in the doorway. They both held their hands at their sides, fists clenched, looking more like each other than I had ever noticed.

"Sara," Binky whispered. "I want a lullaby."

Charles wandered out of his room.

"What's going on?" he asked.

"Go back to bed," my father snapped.

Charles disappeared, an afterthought as always.

Sara came and sat on our bed, displacing our mother, who watched, stricken.

"Hey, little man," Sara said. "What are you scaring me like that for?"

The world warmed around me. Eyelids blinked and drooped. Before they closed, I looked up at her face. Bloodshot eyes— my father was right about the pot. Then darkness, the portal to the outside world shut once more. I was back in the cave with two passageways. My sister's song lilted into the room and then that was gone too. For a moment, there were harsh voices of an argument nearby, but those too receded into silence.

We were alone.

Binky's consciousness drifted back into sleep.

TEN

I WAS ALONE. Or so I thought.

How much damage had I caused? Had Binky had a seizure because of me? I felt my emotions cycle back around to panic. I wondered if I was beginning to be affected mentally by my situation. If somehow the immersion in my younger self's consciousness might influence my ability to act or think rationally.

We slipped back toward deep sleep. I could feel the room go still. The R.E.M. of Binky's eyes sounded like the fluttering of wings. Calming. Soothing. Yet, for me, the panic lurked. I had almost killed us, but I had not finished my task.

I knew that I should not move. I had done enough. But there were two passageways out of this room. I had not explored everywhere. For all I could tell, there were a hundred more rooms in that direction. Roger's voice in my head, telling about the room that led to imagination. He would want me to go there. I had walked through our unconscious and survived. That direction must be where personality and emotion and rational thought and the very basis of our separation from other living things lay. Through that other door waited humanity. The essence of Binky. The essence of me.

The growling had come from that direction. But that menacing rumble must have been a defense mechanism, as clumsy and juvenile as the slime mold curtain and the claustrophobic tunnel. I convinced myself that there could not be a monster living within my younger self's brain.

This situation was all too familiar. It explained why they kept me in therapy and gave me all the drugs that didn't work. To prevent me from doing what I knew was not in my best interests. To quell the urge to complete the task that could be my last. All that time and money, all those chemicals, were aimed at the sole purpose of helping me control that which I could not control.

None of that was here to help me. My excuses seemed plausible. I made myself believe that completing the task was the most important thing. Even as I stood and approached the second passageway, I wondered where in my misfiring brain was the room that had made me this way.

This tunnel did not appear to be long, but there was something obstructing my view. Beyond the object, which nearly reached the ceiling, there was a bright light.

I walked through the portal into the tunnel.

The obstruction in the corridor turned out to be a doorway. It looked like the front door to our house on Sycamore Street. It stood in the exact center of the passageway. I could walk around it on either side. It was moored there, seemingly without purpose.

I tried the doorknob. It was locked.

I walked around to the other side. Again, locked.

A locked door to nowhere.

The bright light down the corridor beckoned me. I followed it and forgot about the door. I walked out into the world. This was not a room, but an infinite space, flowing out in all directions. My feet felt the solid ground below; the rest of me floated above. Everything was distant, blurry. A hundred pastel ovals jostling each other, balloons maybe. A candy-colored playground complete with slides and swings and a roundabout. The sound of crashing waves. Firecrackers. A sunset. The aurora borealis. All contained in this infinite space.

I took a step toward the playground. I needed to get closer to something. The panic had disappeared. I had completed my task and survived. Or so I thought.

The air swirled behind me. I felt it brush the back of my neck. But when I spun around, there was nothing there. Just the passageway back to where I had come from. It wasn't the air. A hiss, behind me again. I twisted my body—no, not my body, myself—and suffered vertigo from the speed of my own movements. But I caught up with it. The sibilance issued from an indistinct mass in front of me. It looked like a cloud of gnats and sounded like a pit of vipers.

GO BACK.

The voice came from everywhere and nowhere. It originated from deep within me, from my lower intestines, my groin. Every syllable hurt.

I did not move. I stared through the cloud. Beyond it, I saw Binky. He sat in front of a giant screen. Images flashed before him, rapidly and subliminally, lighting up his stupefied face. Dreams.

The cloud solidified and shifted in front of me, blocking my view. A winged serpent now, thicker than a tree trunk, stared me down.

WE ARE SLEEPING.

Binky, I said, calling out to my younger self.

The serpent struck, fangs penetrating deep into my forearm. The pain rushed through me, like molten glass in my veins, crystallizing and cutting as it went, opening me up.

I forced myself to push past the agony. The serpent disappeared, replaced by a behemoth covered with red eyes. The giant rose to its full height above me, balancing on claws the size of baseball bats. Its skin oozed pus that burned the ground as it dripped away. It had no mouth, but I could feel it smiling. It enjoyed my pain. I was a plaything and a threat and a curiosity.

The monster leaned toward me, over me. Whatever it was, it was part of Binky.

I am you, I said. *You can't hurt me.*

The eyes blinked at me, out of sync.

WE ARE WE. YOU ARE NOT.

Each of the eyes sprouted into an arm. Each arm held a bladed weapon. Now there was a head atop the body, scarred and aflame. A mouth filled with crooked, jagged teeth. As the knives flashed in my direction, I was convinced the end had arrived.

But the blades never reached me. Instead they taunted me, millimeters away, surrounding me, vibrating with the potential of their devastation.

The creature longed to slash me to ribbons. I could feel it. A part of me wanted that to happen. To savor the satisfaction of unbridled mayhem. But something stopped it.

LET ME.

Buzzing around the monster's head, a small ball of greenish light. It whispered to both of us.

This cannot be done.

The knives around me trembled, then retracted. The monster shrunk, returning to its original form, the cloud of insects. The ball of light rolled over its surface, caressing it. The horrible monster and the beautiful light. My id and superego.

The id objected to the superego, petulantly, like a small child.

WE ARE WE.

Yes. He should not be here.

NOT HERE.

Yes, not here. Take him back. Keep him there.

Before I could understand what had happened, the id engulfed me. I was lifted off my feet and propelled backward. As I flew into the tunnel, I saw Binky. He was still watching the screen. The cloud tossed me back into the empty cave. It was dark and cold. I felt the loss at my core.

YOU ARE HERE.

I laughed at the cloud, at the incongruity of that voice, which left me in agony while spouting shopping mall signage. My levity lasted only a moment.

The id dropped me to the floor. I thought that was it—merely a warning to stay in my place. But then, I felt all my limbs grabbed at once, twisted around me, reformed into a different shape. My consciousness forced order onto my new situation.

I was sitting, my arms hugging my knees, contained in an invisible box about the size of a washing machine. I could not stretch out. I could barely move. That was how my mind discerned it, though I could feel that I had somehow *become* the box. That I was constrained by my own self. It had turned me into my own cage.

And then it was gone.

I was alone. The darkness was complete.

There was nothing else to do but sit there, in the shackles of my own making, waiting for Binky to wake up.

ELEVEN

I HAD ASSUMED that when Binky woke up, I would be freed from my cage. I was wrong. Binky knew my predicament. He deliberated over it in that thoughtful, quiet, scrunched-up way of seven-year-olds, then decided to leave me as I was.

Bound and contained.

As we brushed our teeth.

As we got dressed for school.

As we went down the stairs to the kitchen.

As we poured the Frosted Flakes and the milk.

As we ate.

I'm uncomfortable, I said.

It's easier this way.

It was hard to argue with him. Binky was less skittish with me locked up. Sometime during the night I had massaged the cramps from my legs and shrunk myself to better fit the space. How much simpler this disembodied life could be. If I could let go. But I still chafed at being controlled this way. I bided my time, waiting for my opportunity.

I'd retained unfettered access to the world around me through Binky's senses. Charles loped into the kitchen and fell heavily into the seat next to mine. I wanted to talk to my brother. He had two days left in his freshman year of high school. Already, he was the sullen loner I remembered from later years. I wanted to tell him that he would be successful, that riches were his future. Someday he would be happy and that could make him happier now. I wanted to explain to him that, despite all his desire for payback for his tortured youth, he still shouldn't be an asshole as an adult.

But Binky did not want to talk to Charles and so I remained mute as well. Besides, I realized that I did not know if Charles was happy in his adult life. I knew him only through the occasional profile in a business magazine or the inside sections of the newspaper.

Charles sneered as he grabbed the box of Frosted Flakes. Binky had been working his way slowly through a Tony the Tiger maze on the back. I felt the muscles on our face shift, betraying our hurt.

"It's grrrrrreat," Charles whispered.

He poured some cereal then angled the box out of reach, leaving Binky unable to see the maze and with only the grid of nutritional information to consider.

"After last night …"

"They don't open for another hour."

Whispers had surrounded us all morning. In my parents' room. Outside the bathroom. Now in the hallway approaching the kitchen.

"But you see …"

"I said I'd call."

I'd only been back in time for two days and it was already obvious to me when my father was lying. My parents entered the kitchen together, worlds apart. She looked at us with inconsolable sadness. He, with barely concealed rage.

Coffee was poured. Breakfast prepared. My mother made our lunches, dropping item after item in a perfunctory fashion into brown paper bags. My father stared at nothing we could see with a crushing intensity. Charles seethed. Binky cowered, taking what pleasure he could in the milky, sugary mouthfuls that made my teeth hurt.

"Okay, time to go," our mother said. "The list's here by the phone."

The way she said it, accusatory and expectant, made Charles and Binky perk up. For the first time, they were in the same boat, struck by the fear of having forgotten something important. Then it was clear that she was speaking to our father.

"Lance, the list," she said, tapping the piece of paper on the counter.

He looked at her without remorse or recognition. Our mother took a deep breath.

"You said you'd take Binky shopping this afternoon. To get the stuff he needs for camp."

"I don't think we should call him Binky anymore."

She motioned toward the front door. Charles took the cue and scurried out of the kitchen, tail between his legs, a hyena scared off a carcass by a lion.

"The list is right here."

"I can't."

Binky did not move. We watched them argue.

"You promised."

"I have an appointment."

He stared her down. She didn't blink.

I felt the walls close in around Binky, constricting him. We were both trapped.

Watching her argue and lose made me happy. I couldn't help myself. I couldn't shake the feeling that she was trying to love us. I hated her for wanting to care about me. Because I knew that she didn't. Not enough, anyway. Standing there, facing down my father, she couldn't know how she had abandoned me. She didn't know that when she disappeared it felt like Sara had killed herself all over again. She just didn't know. I hated her for that too.

When my mother didn't return home that day she dropped me off at Columbia, my father called the police. I gave a statement. We watched the news, expecting her to turn up in a ditch somewhere between the Tappan Zee and home. Days passed. Then, the credit card charges started to show up. Upstate. Vermont. Maine. Nova Scotia. Getting farther away. I never knew if my father talked to her. He just told me later that the charges came for a couple of months and then they stopped. She was gone.

I strained against my box. Binky was silent.

"An appointment?" my mother said.

"With Russell," my father said. "That's what you want, isn't it?"

Russell Macauley. The managing partner at my father's law firm. He was going back to work. He was giving up.

My mother's face transported me to that day on the streets of Manhattan, that day she finally abandoned everything. She struggled against the possibility that no matter what she did, she couldn't win.

Sara appeared in the doorway. All morning, she had been unavailable, sequestered behind a closed door. Binky lit up.

"Sara can take me," Binky said, too loudly.

Everyone turned toward us, but our eyes were locked on Sara. I expected the letdown, another request denied, ready again for Binky to fall from such great heights. Then, Sara smiled, saving us.

"Sure thing, little man," she said. "Where are we going?"

"He needs stuff for camp," our father said, holding the list out to Sara.

Binky ran to Sara, wrapping his skinny arms around her waist. She accepted us.

"I just need keys and credit," Sara said, holding us tight.

"Pick him up after school," our mother said. Without another word, without looking at anyone, she headed out of the kitchen.

On the way out to the car, Charles hit Binky hard on the forearm. Our world tasted the sting of salt. Our mother did not notice. She refused to look at us, hiding her own tears.

After we dropped Charles off, I caught her glancing in the rearview mirror, staring at me like a parent digesting the photograph of a dead child.

I recognized the turn for the elementary school. She went straight instead, toward the small strip of stores that we called downtown. She started to cry when we pulled up in front of the bookstore. We sat stone cold in the back seat and watched her shudder, her head drooping toward the steering wheel.

"I'll be right back," she said, managing the words between tears. "I need to get something."

She left us there alone.

Binky strained against his seatbelt, lifting himself ever so slightly in order to get a better view of her walking toward the store entrance.

I had never thought about the bookstore's name: Purgatorio Books. The man who had owned the store—or I should say, still owned it at that moment in 1977—was a Professor emeritus at U Conn. A Dante scholar, he wrote fifteen books about the poet and invested all the paltry royalties into a perpetually failing bookstore. On the door was a sign I had never understood: Abandon all hope, ye who enter here. Binky watched our mother pass under the admonition and inside. The professor's books had a shelf of their own near the front of the store. I remembered them being there even after he died and left the store to my mother, never sold or shelved, a fitting mausoleum to a middling man of letters. My mother was relieved the day the store finally closed, sighing that in all those years, she had barely broke even.

You did this! You made her cry!

Binky's outburst caught me off guard, though not as much as my anger, the vehemence in my response.

You don't know what you're talking about, I said.

You want her to be sad.

He was right and we both knew it. I said nothing.

I think you're the other one. The bad one with the horns and tail.

Before I could respond, there was a tap on our window. Binky cranked it down.

I recognized Conrad, the guy who worked at the bookstore during my entire childhood. I wondered why he stuck around all those years in a dead end job in a dead end town. Thinking back, I figured he was just a lost hippie, someone without the ability to do anything else in the world. Conrad never changed his long stringy hairdo and the kids at my high school used him as a secondary source for weed.

Conrad poked his head through the car window, invading our space. Binky recoiled. The guy smelled of patchouli. I remembered always finding him a bit creepy, too interested in me and my siblings.

"Hey, man," Conrad said. "Your mom's just gotta do something. She'll be right out."

Binky nodded. Conrad grinned, showing us a row of misaligned teeth.

"How's school?" he said.

"Fine," Binky answered.

"Gotta girlfriend?"

Binky shook his head.

"Probably for the best. Girls can be trouble."

Then, he was gone. Conrad backed away from the car, revealing our mother standing behind him. She had pulled herself together. My mother touched Conrad on the arm, then headed around to the driver's door.

Why do you hate her?

I don't hate her, I said.

You said you did.

The imbalance of our relationship struck me again. Here I was, bound in a box, unable to move, trapped with my younger self who could read my mind but allowed me no access to his. I bristled and I felt him back away nervously.

I didn't say it, I said. *I thought it. Sometimes people think things they don't mean when they're angry. Sometimes adults have conflicting emotions.*

You're an adult?

Yes, I said.

I don't understand.

I was growing tired of the many things Binky did not understand.

Our mother adjusted herself in the front seat, sucking in her breath, trying to regain control.

What did she do to you?

She did it to us, I said. *She left me. She's going to leave you.*

I regretted my words immediately. We filled with tears of our own. Nausea swelled within me as Binky vaulted the front seat like a pommel horse. He landed next to our mother and threw himself upon her. How easily he moved, so light and free in this small body. Yet he bore down on our mother with more weight than she could be expected to bear.

"You can't go," Binky said, between sobs.

She pulled us in closer with one arm while wiping away tears with the other hand.

"I have to take you to school, Binky."

"He said you're going to leave me," Binky wailed.

"Who said that?"

Don't tell her, I said. *It's our secret.*

Our mother pushed us away, holding us by the shoulders. Binky looked down at the seat, unable to handle the intensity of her stare.

"Who said that I would leave you?"

"No one," Binky said, unconvincing.

"Was it your father? Did he say that?"

Binky was shaking his head. I wanted to see my mother's face, but he wouldn't look at her. We started to shiver.

"Binky, sometimes adults make decisions …"

Her fingers encircled our chin and forced our head up.

"You know I would never leave you," she said. "No matter what happens, I won't leave you."

Now we were nodding. It pained me to see her lie so unwittingly.

She's not lying. You're the liar.

I said nothing.

She hugged us again. No more tears—just a yearning to stay right in this moment forever.

"It's okay, mommy," Binky said. "Sometimes it's hard for adults."

Her body shook again, with laughter now, and the mood infected us. Binky looked up at her, overcome with the giddiness of having said just the right thing.

She reached over the seat to grab our backpack. Her summer dress clung to her body, stretching as she did. I did some quick math. She had gotten knocked up by my father, her law school boyfriend, when she was a junior in college, just on the far side of twenty years old. All those years, the '60s and the '70s, when she might have been having reckless sex and doing drugs and chanting anti-war slogans at rallies and tripping out at Woodstock, she was trapped raising kids as the wife of an estate lawyer. As tightly as I was shackled in Binky's mind, she was chained by this life.

"We have to go, Binky," she said. "You can sit up here with me."

Binky lay down on the front seat and put his head in her lap. She pulled away from the store, steering with one hand and playing with our hair with the other. That was how we stayed for the duration of the drive until finally we slowed again and came to a gentle stop.

For a long moment, nothing moved. Then, she spoke.

"Go," she said, her voice barely a whisper. "Don't be late."

TWELVE

BINKY SWITCHED TO autopilot, making his smooth approach to Ms. Mittewag's classroom. I was lost in my own thoughts as well. Neither of us noticed that the halls were empty, that we were late. Not until someone grabbed us and tossed us up against the lockers.

All systems went on alert. When the world stopped spinning, we saw three fifth graders surrounding us. They looked unhappy and really big.

Only one of them talked. The other two were muscle.

"My brother said you were saying some stuff at lunch yesterday. Was that you?"

I relaxed. The kid had left us an exit as big as a warehouse. All we had to do was say no and we'd be on our way.

Binky nodded his head yes.

The fifth grader leaned in closer. This was it. The classic moment where the geeky little kid gets terrorized by the bully. Something unpleasant was coming—getting stuffed in a locker or a wedgie, maybe a head stuffed into a toilet or just a good old-fashioned beating. Binky heard what I was thinking; he agreed that we were screwed. We made a weak, ineffective attempt to wiggle away, like a plastic bag stuck in a tree on a windy day.

"He said you knew stuff," the boy said. "I wanna know something."

The boy's face was so close to us I could smell his breakfast. Cherry Pop Tarts.

He didn't look angry. Curious, maybe. Embarrassed.

"What's a blow job?" he whispered.

Binky turned to me, looking for salvation in my answer. I said nothing.

"I told you he didn't know," another boy said.

"Shut up."

The bully leaned into us, crushing Binky into the locker. His eyes pled with us. He didn't want to beat us up, not today. He wanted the answer.

What's a blow job?

First, let me go, I said. *Let me out of this box.*

He's hurting me.

I know, I said. *Let me go.*

Then I was free. All restraints dissolved. I stretched out and looked into the face of the fifth grader.

"Tell me," he said.

I gave Binky a heterosexual version of the act, taking care with the pronouns, and my younger self repeated it word for word.

The bigger kids backed off. It must have been the clinical nature of the description that pushed them away. Or maybe the confidence with which it was delivered, despite our squeaky voice. Respect had been earned. Awe, even. There was no questioning Binky's authority on the matter.

The fifth graders retreated to their classroom, leaving us alone in the hallway. Flush with victory, Binky hurried to Ms. Mittewag's room. There, the kids were all still settling in for the day. As we walked back to our seat, I could feel their eyes upon us. All of them admiring, wondering.

Ms. Mittewag had given up completely at this point. The lights went off, the TV on. A morning of *The Electric Company* and whatever else was on PBS.

But we barely watched any of it. Throughout the morning, the notes weaved their way back to us, like pilgrims on the trail to Canterbury, each one a question and a story.

I spent the morning dictating to Binky, spelling each word as he painstakingly transcribed answers on the notes. We would finish one and pass it back into the crowd, only to turn to the next one.

A wide range of predictable questions. There were the basic mechanics questions, of course—you stick what where? Then, there were the urban legends—can you really get pregnant from a toilet seat? We provided correct definitions to words that only sounded dirty, like uvula and epidermis. We answered each one diligently with a minimum of four-letter words. Occasionally, I tailored the content to the age of my audience, but on the whole I just remained blissfully content with the inappropriateness of this endeavor.

It was out on the playground, however, that Binky and I understood the full scope of our newfound celebrity. We were approached by kids from all grades, a constant stream of believers paying their respects as if we were the Godfather. The questions got more sophisticated, but only marginally so. Our answers were, of course, well received and greatly appreciated.

As Binky soaked up the attention and I dispensed the wisdom, I realized just how isolated I had been in elementary school. I thought I had friends. If you had asked me, I might have even said I was a popular kid. But now I understood that I was the quiet kid in the corner, the one who always thought he was in the mix but who was actually invisible. As we swam upstream, into the bigger pond of high school, I did find likeminded kids to hang out with, but even then I was always on the fringe, more observer than participant.

In one day, I had changed all that for Binky. He was smack in the middle of the social elite right now. He was getting a taste of sweet acceptance and I wondered if now it would hurt that much more to lose it.

The second morning period after recess continued much the same. Lunch as well. The supply of questions seemed endless. But I had yet to be stumped.

I thought nothing could stop us.

And then, after lunch, we went to gym.

"This is our last class together, so you decide what we play," Mr. Hartford said.

I remembered his crew cut correctly. But, in my memory, the rest of my former gym teacher had been remade to fit what he should have been. If you had asked me to describe him, I might have said that he was mid-fifties, tall, with limbs like steel pipes, exhibiting prominent scars from some distant war. That was the drill sergeant I recalled.

But Mr. Hartford shared only the crew cut with that image. Otherwise, he was young, barely mid-twenties. I was beginning to wonder how I got a decent education when my school had been staffed by teachers barely out of their teens. And he was skinny. Not wiry or ropy—skinny. I could detect no muscle definition whatsoever. Still, the kids all sat on the floor in front of him in fear. He had a big voice. We were blinded by the crew cut. Only mean people had crew cuts.

"We'll put it to a vote. Square dancing?"

All the girls raised their hands. I did a quick count of the gender breakdown of the class, and understood that the election was fixed.

"Twelve for dancing. Dodgeball?"

All the boys raised their hands. Binky fell in line, not a moment's hesitation.

"Fourteen. Line up against the wall to divide up teams."

We counted off ones and twos, then took our sides, thirteen of us on each end of the basketball court. I looked around the gymnasium, spotting the various torture devices—the chin-up bar, the climbing rope, the wrestling mat—but I found nowhere to hide.

Binky breathed in short gasps, a rabbit frozen by the glare of a wolf.

We had an advantage this time. I had years of experience with such games. Years of being pummeled and outplayed. I could help Binky with the strategy. Knowledge would be our power.

Binky, I said. *Here's what to do. Stay back at the free throw line and lob balls up high. That'll confuse the other guys and let your teammates nail them.*

Okay.

Really, just stay halfway back. It'll be easy to see the incoming balls. You can dodge. Or even catch them and put them out. You got it?

Okay, I got it.

I suddenly had visions of a conclusion to this game that had never happened before. We could be the last kid standing. If we just followed a simple strategy. Lay low. Provide cover. Stay alert.

Binky and I could win this thing. I wanted to win.

"Balls in!" Mr. Hartford shouted.

The whistle blew. Mr. Hartford dumped over a hamper, and twenty red-rubber balls bounced into the field of play. Kids, mostly boys but a couple of girls as well, darted from the back line toward the balls. The cavernous room filled with shrieks, shouts, and squeaky sneakers.

Binky also ran. I could tell that it was hard for him, maintaining an even speed and steady posture. The faster he went the more we listed and swayed, like an errant satellite threatening to break orbit and careen helplessly into deep space. He scurried past the free throw line, not even a pause.

No, I said. *The free throw line. Go back. You'll be a sitting duck any closer.*

Binky skidded to a stop, nearly falling over. A ball bounced toward us.

Get the ball, I shouted.

Again, too quick a pivot. This time Binky did fall. The ball rolled past us.

Never mind, I said. *Get back.*

All the balls had been grabbed by eager hands now. Streaks of red buzzed all around us, thrown at varying velocities.

Binky scrambled back to his feet and hurried toward the free throw line. He ran right past it again.

What are you doing? I screamed. *The free throw line!*

I felt myself losing my grip. So many memories of so many failed attempts to hold my own in sporting events flashed by.

I don't know what the free throw line is.

The line you just ran past, I said. *Go back!*

Binky did as he was told. This time he found it, planting his feet firmly where I told him to. He stared at the line, to the exclusion of everything else. A ball whizzed past, barely missing us.

Look up, I said. *Damnit, Binky, you've got to pay attention to the balls!*

You said we'd be safe here.

I said you'd have to dodge. Or catch the ball. Look out! Duck!

Binky was on the ground again. He didn't dodge so much as tumble out of the way. I felt the twinge of pain in our elbow where it hit the floor.

Come on, I shouted. *You can do better than that. Get that ball!*

A ball rolled past us. Binky reached out too late and missed it.

Damnit, get up, I said. *Come on.*

Stop yelling at me.

I'm not yelling, I said. *I'm helping you out.*

You're yelling.

Okay, sorry, I said. *Just stand up. Pay attention.*

The bleachers were filling up as kids went out. Mr. Hartford would call the names as they got hit. The weak had been culled from the herd. Now it was mainly the swift and sure-handed left on the court. And Binky.

See? Our strategy is working, I said. *You're out of the way, so you're not out yet.*

I don't like this game.

Another ball rolled toward us.

Grab it, Binky, I said.

He lunged and this time he grabbed it. We squeezed it, testing the pressure inside. It felt good, taking a small measure of our own fate into our hands.

Okay, good, I said. *See that boy over there? In the green shirt. Toss this ball high at him. When he looks to catch it, someone else will nail him.*

Aren't we out if he catches it?

I had forgotten that rule. I didn't want to be out. I suddenly felt victory within our grasp. Somewhere, I heard Roger laughing at me. But I didn't care.

Right, right, I said. *Okay, toss it high, but over his head so he can't catch it.* As Binky wound up to throw the ball, I knew that this plan was not going to work. The ball felt much heavier than it should have. Our muscles struggled to bring it back behind our head. As he thrust his arm forward, like a slingshot, I could tell that he didn't have a grip on the ball, that he wasn't able to work out the trajectory we had discussed.

The ball left Binky's hand, a lame duck, fluttering only a few feet before it bounced off Matt Ferguson's thick skull. Matt was on our team.

He turned on us. I knew my run for glory had come to an end. Despite being our teammate, Matt hurled a ball into our stomach. We doubled over, gasping. Matt hovered over us.

"Get in the game," he said.

He lifted us up and carried us to the front line. Two boys on the other side, Matt's friends, waited for him to drop us. They nailed us good—one in the head and one in the side. Binky did not move, struggling to recover his breath from Matt's opening shot.

"Benedict, out!" Mr. Hartford called. "Hurry up. Off the court."

Binky mustered the strength to limp off the court to the bleachers.

What the hell was that? I said. *Were you even trying?*

Binky was silent. With the last of the dead weight gone, the intensity on the court rose, the real competition began. I stewed on the sidelines. Binky gave me the silent treatment.

"Is it true what they're saying?" a voice behind us whispered. "That you know stuff."

I hadn't realized that we had sat down in front of Missy O'Neill.

"I guess so," Binky said.

Missy leaned forward, nearly resting her chin on our shoulder. Her warm breath on our neck made us ticklish and tingly.

"Does it hurt?" she said. "My sister said it hurts when you do it."

Binky repeated what I told him. By now, he didn't hesitate. It was almost as if I was speaking myself, though I knew that wasn't true.

"It hurts for girls the first couple of times," Binky said. "But then, it can feel really good. Not as easily as for boys. But with the right person and some practice."

Missy held her breath as Binky talked, exhaling only when he fell silent.

"Thanks," she said.

She retreated from us. The ticklish, tingly feeling gone, I sensed Binky trying to figure out how to regain that contact.

You need to tell her exactly what I say.

Binky turned around to face Missy. She wasn't ugly. She never was. But they made her believe their lies.

"Missy," Binky said.

His tone, so paternal and sincere, drew her in again.

"Don't let them tell you you're not beautiful, okay?" he said. "It's not true. But they'll say it if you let them."

Missy's face crumpled in on itself, trying to understand. I wondered if she heard anything except "you're not beautiful."

"You don't have to do what boys tell you. They don't need you to do it. They won't like you just because you do it."

"What?"

She could only form that simple question. An utter indictment of my crudely formed plan to save her from herself. The confusion she felt only made me more determined.

"Sex should be saved for someone you love. Someone who deserves you. Do you understand?"

I could see that she didn't. How could she?

Why are we saying this? She looks scared.

There was nothing more I could do. The only thing left to say was the blunt warning. I could only hope that it would be so odd as to stick in her head for the next half decade, an indecipherable riddle that would suddenly become clear at the exact moment it was needed.

Tell her not to sleep with Louis Kirk, I said.

Why?

Just tell her!

"He wants me to tell you not to sleep with Louis Kirk," Binky said.

We turned away from Missy's confused fear. Binky could not stand her looking at him like a freak. Not after her breath on his neck had opened up a new window for him on the possibilities of intimate contact.

As we fell back into silence, I could feel him thinking about her. Probably wondering what it would be like to breathe on Missy's neck. To touch her hair. To hug her. I searched for an indication that Binky had any sense of our future preferences, but he was still closed off to me. I suspected that there was just an amorphous need, an unformed desire, the vague inkling that contact with someone else might lead to pleasure.

In some few ways, it is easier to be seven years old.

"Benedict," Mr. Hartford shouted. "You're wanted in the Principal's office!"

The secretary from the front office was standing next to the gym teacher. With a withered bony finger, she beckoned for us to come with her.

THIRTEEN

WE SAT OUTSIDE the Principal's office on a hard wooden bench for three long minutes. I could hear Binky pacing back and forth inside the cave, rolling side to side like a metronome. He did not talk to me, but I knew he blamed me for everything. I wanted to tell him that getting called to the Principal's office was a good thing, a badge of honor among the elementary school set, even though I knew it wouldn't help. Binky didn't want to talk to me; the chill made that clear.

"Benedict," the shriveled secretary barked. "Principal Vanderbilt will see you now."

It was comforting that my memory of Principal Vanderbilt matched the reality exactly. A sixty-something balding man with a paunch and a '70s porno mustache. When someone says the word "principal," I think of him.

He was not alone in the office. Ms. Mittewag was there as well. She looked concerned. Vanderbilt put on his practiced stern expression. It worked on Binky, who shrunk deeper into his chair, but I could see that Vanderbilt's face, from eyebrows to jowls, had frayed around the edges from years of foisting this very look upon generations of children. The severity was a façade. Nothing real to fear here. There was a third person in the room. A woman wearing all white, young and a bit plump, with a round kind face. She was the type of girl who would have been my friend in high school. Probably the school nurse.

"Benedict, do you know why you're here?" Vanderbilt said.

His question sounded like an accusation. Binky shook his head. An honest response for him and a flat out lie for me.

"You've been talking to the other kids," he said. "Telling them things."

I felt our face flush, telegraphing our guilt. I could hardly fault Binky for that. Going beet red at the slightest provocation is one of my best party tricks.

"These things you've been saying. They're not appropriate for a child to talk about. Do you understand?"

"Or write," Ms. Mittewag said. "Who told you these things?"

Ms. Mittewag punctuated her question by dropping a handful of notes onto the Principal's desk, each one containing a bite of the forbidden fruit.

"Tell us, Benedict," Vanderbilt said, leaning forward and filling our vision. "Someone must have told you these things. Who was it?"

Binky didn't answer.

Principal Vanderbilt sat back again. He paged through our file.

"You have siblings. An older brother. Did he tell you those things?"

Binky remained silent.

"Or your sister maybe. Sara. I remember her."

"No!"

Binky didn't mean to shout, but there is no controlling an eruption of loyalty.

"It wasn't your sister?"

"No."

Binky paused.

Don't tell them the truth, I said.

He ignored me.

"It was him. He told me."

"So it was your brother," Vanderbilt said. He checked the file again. "Charles."

"No, not him," Binky said, his voice sinking deep into quicksand.

The room grew quiet. The three adults exchanged glances. Principal Vanderbilt came out from behind the desk. He took a seat next to us.

"You can tell us the truth here. This is a safe place. Have you been talking to another adult? A man? Someone you don't know?"

"No. Not ... I don't know. I ..."

Binky didn't have the words. The room filled with dread, three adults wondering if something horrible had happened on their watch.

They think you've been talking to strangers, I said.

I don't talk to strangers.

Tell them that.

But I talk to you. I don't know you.

You do know me, I said. *You know you do.*

I guess.

Tell them Charles told you.

That's a lie.

Sometimes you need to lie.

"Benedict, are you okay? Benedict?"

We focused on the room again. The nurse was kneeling down in front of us now. She had a hand on our forehead and looked deeply into our eyes.

Binky nodded at her and she could not hide her relief.

"It was Charles," Binky said. "He told me."

Again, the adults spoke wordlessly, assessing the situation. Principal Vanderbilt wanted to discuss with the nurse. Ms. Mittewag took Binky's hand and led him out of the room.

I shouldn't have done that.

No, I said. *It's okay. Better this way.*

We paused in the outer office.

"No luck getting his parents," the secretary said.

"There's only one period left," Ms. Mittewag said. "Tell Jack I'm taking him back to class. I'll talk to his dad when he picks him up."

We walked silently back to the classroom.

No. It's not better. It's lying. It's bad. You do bad things.

Sometimes things seem bad when they aren't, I said.

Stop saying that. You are bad. I don't like you. You want to hurt Sara. You hate Mommy. You tell me to say grown-up things that get me in trouble. You tell me to lie.

We arrived back in our classroom. Ms. Mittewag led us back to our desk. The other kids had not returned from gym yet. We were alone. She knelt next to us, still holding our hand.

"Ben, you can tell me what's bothering you," she said. "It's okay."

In her eyes, I saw the teacher that she would become, the one I wished had taught me. Binky saw her too.

I need to protect Sara.

Binky was right, of course. That had to be why I was here. To help Sara. To protect her. Only then did I realize that I had been hoping that I wouldn't have to do anything. I still felt that way. Maybe my mere presence here had changed things. Maybe I could stop the rape from happening just by existing.

I need to protect everyone from you.

I'm not the problem.

But I could feel that Binky had left, vacating the cave for another part of the brain where I couldn't follow. I wondered if he could hear me, if he would even listen.

Please, Binky, I said. *Don't.*

"Ben?" Ms. Mittewag said. "Can you hear me?"

"He talks to me," Binky said in a whisper, maybe hoping I wouldn't hear.

"Who talks to you?"

"I don't know. He says that he's me."

"Is this a person?"

"No. I don't know."

Don't tell her, I said. *Please, Binky.*

My words echoed around me, too late and without strength.

"Is it just someone you hear? Someone who talks to you in your head? A voice?"

Binky lunged for her and she took him into her arms. He whispered into her ear.

"He says things. He says someone is going to hurt Sara. He scares me."

I said nothing. There was nothing left to say.

"It's okay. It's okay."

"I just want him to go away."

On that sentiment, we were in complete agreement.

FOURTEEN

I FELT AS if I had been dipped in liquid nitrogen, flash frozen; every time I bent my fingers, attempting to make a fist, the digits snapped off at the knuckles, cracking like dry twigs, before growing back, only to solidify anew. Binky had abandoned me. I didn't know if he would come back to the cave. I shivered and waited.

At the end of the school day, Ms. Mittewag stood with us outside. Most of the other kids had cleared out by the time Sara pulled up in front of the school. I could see Charles sitting sullen in the front seat. Sara got out and ran toward us, radiant. Her mere presence warmed us, much to my relief.

"Sorry I'm late," she said. "Traffic."

Ms. Mittewag looked concerned, unwilling to pass Binky into the care of this young girl. Sara steeled herself, giving Binky's teacher a look that said she knew they were not that many years apart.

"We tried to call your parents," Ms. Mittewag said. "Please tell them we need to talk to them."

"What did you do?" Sara said playfully to Binky, tousling his hair. "Is my Binky getting into trouble?"

"This is serious," Ms. Mittewag said. "Tell them to call me or Principal Vanderbilt as soon as possible."

"I got it," Sara said sharply. "Lay off the kid. Whatever he did, I'm sure it's no big deal. Let's go, Bink."

Sara grabbed our hand and pulled us away. Her words had shattered the bonds that tethered us to the school, allowing us to bob away like a bottle tossed into the ocean. Binky calmed—everything he had ever done was okay. I was allowed to thaw out just a bit more.

As we climbed into the back seat, we watched Ms. Mittewag watch us. We drove off, leaving our teacher standing alone.

"Your teacher's gotta stick up her ass, huh Binky?" Sara said.

She swerved into the other lane and skidded through a left turn on a yellow light.

"Learn to drive, will ya?" Charles said, only half kidding. "You trying to kill us?"

"Only you, jerkoff," Sara said with a laugh. "If I hit the pole just right, I can send you through the windshield and leave me and Binky unscathed. They'll teach you that in Driver's Ed next year."

Charles gave her the finger.

"Do that again and I'll cut it off." Sara looked at us in the rearview mirror. "I'm just kidding, Binky. Don't worry."

"She won't cut my finger off," Charles said.

"No, I meant about the pole. Your finger's mine."

"Fuck you."

"Big words for a freshman."

"Small words, actually. One syllable each. You know what a syllable is, right?"

Sara jabbed quickly and unexpectedly, nailing Charles in the ribs before he could block her. He grunted, then fell silent, unwilling to show that she'd hurt him and unable to talk without betraying himself.

"So, little man," Sara called back to us. "It's about time for you to get in some trouble. Take the pressure off the rest of us. What'd you do?"

Binky beamed at the implication that he was helping his sister. He caught Sara's eyes in the rearview mirror and smiled at her. That was enough for both of them.

"He's not in real trouble," Charles said, having caught his breath. "He's too wussy."

"Binky's not you," Sara said. She pulled the car up to the curb in front of our house. "Get out."

"I thought we were going to the mall," Charles said.

"Binky and I are going to the mall. You got your key?"

"Yeah, I got my key."

He huffed out of the car. We sped off.

Sara flipped on the radio. "I'm Your Boogie Man" by KC and the Sunshine Band. I had a friend who tortured us with that song when he was making a mix for his divinely inspired Disco Halloween party. Static filled the car as Sara scanned for a new station.

"Repeat after me. Disco sucks."

"Disco sucks."

She scrolled past a snippet of a voice, then had to roll the dial back slowly to hit the frequency just right. "Fly Like an Eagle"—Steve Miller Band. Sara returned her hand to the wheel, satisfied.

Sara sang along with the radio, increasing my agitation. As the song said, time was slipping away.

I had been here for nearly two days. Thirty-six hours without doing anything to prevent the tragedy that was coming. I was the lone sailor in the crow's nest and I had been ousted from my position just before the rocks along the shore appeared. It was worse than that. I was mute, unable to sound the alarm, and I had pushed the boy with the voice overboard. I tried to sense Binky, but I couldn't find him. Now was the time. We were alone with Sara. I had no voice and my younger self thought I was the enemy.

I did the only thing I could think of. I screamed.

Binky! I shouted. *Get out here!*

The shell of petrified wood that surrounded me cracked and fell to the ground.

Binky! We have to tell her!

No response. My anger created its own heat, scorching the floor at my feet.

They're going to hurt her, I said. *Z and his friends. Righetti and that Jackson kid.*

Binky stared at the back of the front seat. He traced the lines in the upholstery with his eyes. I could tell he was trying not to listen to me, but he heard every word.

It's going to happen at the party Thursday night, I said. *Unless we tell her.*

Stop it! I'm not listening to you.

Let me talk to her, Binky, I said. *Give me your voice.*

Even I was surprised I said that. I wasn't even sure such a thing was possible. Binky had fallen silent again, turning our world into a perfect vacuum. I struggled to breathe.

You're trying to make me do stuff again. I won't do it.

It'll be your fault if something happens, I said.

"Binky, are you okay?"

The car had stopped. Sara peered over the front seat at us.

"I don't want them to hurt you."

"Oh, Bink. No one's gonna hurt me."

Outside the car, I could hear other voices, but Binky would not look away from Sara. Four teenage girls were descending on the car.

"Come on up. Sit next to me."

The funk forgotten, Binky scrambled over the seat. Doors opened. The volume in the car rose to one notch below deafening. One girl got in the front, forcing us closer to Sara. The others clambered into the back, jostling three across to get comfortable. Five competing perfumes threatened to make us gag.

"Okay, ladies, thank Binky here for making this trip possible."

In unison sing-song, the girls chanted, "Thank you, Binky," then broke into laughter. The girl next to us grabbed Binky and kissed him on each cheek. All the blood flowed into our face, drawn magnetically to the crescent imprints left by her lips.

We were off to the mall. Another opportunity to change the future missed. I felt Binky pushing me away, determined in his unrelenting immature certitude to ignore me.

FIFTEEN

"I'M GONNA DO it," Sara said.

"With X?"

"Who else would I do it with?"

"I don't know. Anyone."

"X loves me. Those other guys just see tits and ass. X sees my soul."

As she talked, Sara turned her half-naked body sideways to the mirror, taking in the curves that attracted the boys.

We were crammed into the dressing room with Sara and Angela, the other girl from the front seat, the one who kissed Binky. The rest of the gaggle disappeared at the first sight of boys to hang out with. Sara wanted to shop for an outfit for the party Thursday and Angela wanted to hang with Sara and Binky was part of the package deal.

Binky and I sat on the small seat in the corner of the dressing room, watching Angela and Sara try on skimpy tops. Sara picked up a yellow sarong with beaded fringe.

"What about this one, Bink?"

He shook his head.

"Good call," Angela said. "Makes you look like a canary."

They both laughed, though Sara made Angela wait for a moment before letting her know that she got the joke.

"Do you love X?" Angela said.

Sara dropped her top to the floor. Angela had asked exactly the question I wanted to ask. Watching Sara there, hands on hips, wearing only a bra and skirt, I had a vision of the two of us—Sara and her gay brother—hitting the boutiques of Manhattan. She would have liked that.

I wanted that to be our future.

"Of course I love him," she said.

Angela and Binky were convinced. I believed that she believed it, but I was terribly frustrated at being the only adult in a dressing room full of children. This situation called for a parent, not a friend. I was experiencing all the horror of watching your child slip away.

I'd almost had a daughter.

When Roger called that afternoon, I had been standing at the window, looking down on the busy street. I was out sick that day, just a coincidence. It happened sometimes. Not often, but occasionally a task arose first thing in the morning and the panic wouldn't let me leave the apartment. On that day, by the time I had finished alphabetizing all our books and put them back on the shelves, by the time I could breathe normally again, it seemed like too much work to head uptown. It had just started to snow. I distinctly remember being happy that I wasn't going anywhere.

"It's a girl," he said.

Guatemala must have come through. I don't know what I was thinking. Everyone had told me that adoptions were an unlikely proposition. Particularly for gay men. The process could take years even with the right connections and the right lies—that was the conventional wisdom. So I had let Roger wear me down. I let him put in the various applications. I went to the meetings and charmed the necessary managers and officials. If he put a document in front of me, I signed it.

It made Roger so happy that each time I complied willingly. I never believed the adoption would happen. Even when the guest bedroom was stocked with toys and diapers and baby furniture. Even when he showed me the mockup of the baby announcement on the computer, missing only a name and key stats. Even when he told his parents.

On that snowy New York day, I listened and said nothing.

"We're pregnant! I'm going into labor!"

He might as well have been in the room with me. I felt everything he would have done. Roger would have grabbed me by the shoulders and given me a little shake. Then his hands would have wandered up to the back of my neck, pulling me toward him. He would have kissed me and whispered, "It's okay."

"We're on an eight o'clock flight from LaGuardia to Houston. We'll be in Guatemala City in the morning. I'm going straight from work."

He would have pulled me in, letting the full length of his body press against mine. I would have put my head on his shoulder.

If he had been home, I would have gone to the airport.

"I've got to go," I lied.

"Okay. I'll see you at the airport." Roger paused. "I love you."

"I love you too."

And I meant it, despite what I did.

We heard him coughing. When we came into the store, there had been a man sitting on one of the chairs outside the dressing room, a young guy waiting impatiently for his wife to finish shopping. With his eyes, he had pawed at Angela and Sara—mostly Sara. I could feel him out there, trying to develop X-ray vision and see through the thin door of the dressing stall, hanging on every word.

I heard the door next to us open.

"Harold? What about this one?"

"Uh, yeah. Yeah, it's great."

"You're not even looking."

"I said it's great."

The door next to ours latched shut again. Sara gave Angela a sly glance.

"What?"

"Take off your shirt. Let's have some fun with the asshole."

Angela looked confused, but she pulled her top off. The two of them checked the positioning of their bras in the mirror. Sara opened the door to the dressing stall and pulled Angela out.

"Harold. Which do you like better?" Sara pointed to her bra first, then Angela's. "The red or the blue?"

Through the door, I saw Harold shift uncomfortably in his chair. He stared right at their breasts. No danger of him not looking this time.

"Come on, Harold," Sara said. "You must have an opinion."

Then the stranger did something that sickened me. He smiled.

"The red one. Definitely."

"Harold!" his wife shouted, coming out of her stall. "What are you doing?"

"Thanks," Sara said, pushing Angela back into our changing room. "You're a doll, Harold."

Sara closed the door behind them, but not before she made sure Harold saw her unlatching her bra.

I heard the man and his wife leaving the store hastily. They would fight all the way home, I was sure of it. I felt nauseated. Sara was so free, so certain in her own safety. I didn't want her to change and I knew she had to. The contradictions made me dizzy. I wanted to tell her that confidence alone couldn't protect her.

"Your brother doesn't look so good," Angela said.

"Binky, you okay?" Sara said.

"I feel sick."

"Don't let him throw up," Angela said. "I hate vomit."

"Shut up, Angela. You feel like you're gonna barf?"

"I don't know. Maybe."

Angela was already dressed and out the door. Sara pulled on her top and took our hand.

"Sorry about that, little man," Sara said. "Let's try some ginger ale."

She led us out into the main store.

"I shouldn't do things like that," Sara said.

"No, you shouldn't," Binky said.

For a moment, I thought that maybe I had done it. That sounded like my voice, like what I wanted to say. I yearned for that moment to be enough to change everything, but knew without a doubt that it wasn't.

In the months before my betrayal, Roger had talked incessantly about names. He was a mass of indecision, changing his preferences from moment to moment. I had no suggestions to offer, only jokes. How about Rover? Moon Unit? He laughed, but he should have known. He probably did. But Roger could be so blindly optimistic at times.

I finally sent him a text message at 7:30 that night. I had been ignoring his calls to the cell and home phone, not to mention emails and texts. But by 7:30 the constant ringing had stopped. The text I sent was brief—something impersonal like "we need 2 talk"—and I knew that I was salting the wound. I actually believed that he had brought this on himself. He would come home. We would fight and we would see where we were after that.

Roger didn't come home from the airport. He got on the plane and went to Guatemala without me. He had already arranged for two months off from work. He left me in the wintry city and roamed Central and South America alone. Of course, he didn't pick up our daughter. Roger closed that door when he landed, contacting the adoption agency to let them know what had happened. That was Roger, ever diligent. He sent me updates on where he was—Costa Rica, Peru, Brazil,

Argentina, Chile—and I went about my own life, waiting.

Then, he came home, packed up all his stuff, and left me. Roger let me keep the apartment. In my mind, I ended the relationship, but it was Roger who walked away.

Binky sucked on his straw. The ginger ale was too syrupy, but it calmed him. We had found the other three girls and now the five of them held court in the main atrium as boys circled them like moons. Sara was clearly the center of attention—the other girls followed her lead. Even as she flirted and rebuffed, her eyes constantly darted around the mall, looking for someone else.

"Did he say he'd be here?" Angela said.

"Yeah," Sara said. "Prick."

"Maybe he got caught up with his brother."

"Yeah. Maybe."

The mention of Z softened Sara, but I couldn't read her beyond the superficial change. Binky slurped up the last of the ginger ale, announcing the end of his drink with a loud static as he got nothing but air.

"My parents'll kill me if I don't get the stuff on this list."

Sara waved Binky's camp list in the air like a handkerchief.

"They'll find another reason to kill you even if you do get it."

"Yeah. Too true."

Sara hopped off the table and took Binky by the hand.

"Feeling better, little man?" she asked.

Binky nodded. I was amazed once more at his ability to shift gears, to shuttle from emotion to emotion effortlessly, toggling between feelings as easily as changing his shoes.

I was still wracked, but my ability to affect my younger self remained elusive. I was growing tired of riding shotgun in this life. As we returned to Sears, this time to the boys' department, I wondered what it would take to get my message across.

I was running out of time.

SIXTEEN

WE DROPPED ANGELA off at her house. The rest of the girls stayed behind—plenty of rides to be had at the mall. I tried to picture their faces and remember their names. Nothing but blanks.

Sara left the radio off as we pulled away again. With Angela gone, I moved over toward the door. I was still in the front seat, but there was distance between us now. Sara chewed on her pinky nail as she drove, a habit that became her unfortunate signature, gnawing to draw blood, in the short time left to her after the rape.

"You're not gonna be like them," she said.

Binky and I both felt as if she was talking to us, and maybe we were both right. We stared at her, Binky's unwieldy love weighing down his small frame. Combined with my own burden, our density grew nearly unmanageable, threatening to turn into a black hole that sucked the world into oblivion.

"Not you, Bink. You're gonna be one of the good ones."

"X is a good one," Binky said. "You said he's the one."

Sara laughed

"Yeah. Yeah, I guess so."

She moved to her next nail, having ripped a significant sliver of the last one off between her teeth.

What I did next was cruel, but I was tired of being ignored. I knew I couldn't hide my thoughts from Binky. So I went to the other extreme. I projected my memories against the wall, forty feet high, IMAX with surround sound. Any pretense of defenses was dropped. I wanted him to see the future.

I started with the image of Sara dead in her coffin, even though it was something I had never witnessed myself.

The day of Sara's funeral, my parents told me to stay home with Charles. I wanted to go to the service. But they said no. I heard my mother tell my father that it was going to be a media circus, no place for children. Charles was seventeen, the same age Sara had been when she was raped. Still a child in my mother's eyes, he didn't mind staying behind. He let the excuse that someone needed to watch me carry the day.

All the newspapers covered the funeral. The TV stations all sent cameras. The rape and trial had been big news in our neck of the woods. In the immediate aftermath, the lurid crime coverage had turned into hand-wringing what-is-wrong-with-our-children stories. Then, they left it alone for a year, moving on to fresher blood, until the trial, when they repeated the progression again, squeezing at least five news cycles out of the story. When Sara killed herself, we braced for one more run at this trough. The media did not disappoint.

I argued that I was old enough to attend. Rarely did I have the strength to pit my youthful indignation against my parents' infinite sadness. It was impossible to fight with them. All emotion drowned before it could be heard. Sara was dead and I wanted to say goodbye. I thrashed and screamed. I begged and bargained. They ignored me.

When they closed the door behind them—leaving me on the stairs, watching them go—I cried.

Charles came out of the kitchen. I braced for the taunts. They didn't come. Instead, he looked at me and I recognized that expression. The same one he wore in those late June days when the phone never stopped ringing and Sara wouldn't come out of her room. At first I mistook the strain as anger over what had happened, but it was more than that. There was a deep sense of responsibility in the creases around his eyes. As our parents left us alone in the house on the day of my sister's funeral, I saw that look again. He did not say a word to me. He put a hand on my shoulder and drifted past me up the stairs. He left me behind and shut himself in his room.

Maybe they understood what they were doing. My mother and father did not want me to say goodbye that day because they knew I would see Sara again. Maybe they knew I'd have a second chance.

"She's not dead," Binky said.

Sara turned to him. We had stopped again.

"What, Binky?"

"He wants me to talk to you."

I knew that he had been there with me, watching us sit on the stairs. Binky knew what a funeral was.

"We can talk about whatever you want on the way home," she said. "I just need to do something here."

Sara motioned to a large house. We were in one of the rich neighborhoods. I had friends over this way in high school and I always envied what they had. The mansion we looked at now could eat our little ranch house as an appetizer.

X's house.

Sara took the keys out of the ignition and got out. Binky scurried to keep up with her as she strode toward the front door.

X and Z's dad owned a successful car dealership. That had been one of the dwelt-upon ironies of the crime. Everyone wanted the rapists to be lowlifes. Well, they were lowlifes; it's just that no one expected them to be rich lowlifes.

X answered the door.

I knew why Sara loved him. I loved him too.

We shared a type.

Roger had been everything that I wasn't attracted to. He was steady and stable. Not ugly, but wholly conventional. Roger displayed confidence and understood what he wanted. He was unbroken.

Not so with X. This is the guy I would have wanted to talk to in a bar, the one I would never have known how to approach. His hair was messed-up, a glorious tangle of chaos, not like the planned disarray of the over-moussed phonies. He gazed at my sister with deep blue eyes. X diminished his average height with a permanent slouch. This boy needed to be fixed. The appeal was undeniable.

"Hey," X said.

"Hey yourself," Sara said.

X backed up and let us in.

"What's the kid doing here?"

"The kid was at the mall with me," Sara said. "Where were you?"

"Yeah."

X let the silence surround them. He didn't lie or apologize. It reminded me of my father. Like my mother, Sara waited. The moment gripped our stomach and twisted, leaving me wondering in a fit of fear just how much of our lives actually are predestined.

Sara was not my mother.

She hit X on the arm, having no interest in letting the moment slide. We were all surprised when X recoiled in pain. I didn't think she'd hit him that hard, and the look on Sara's face showed that she agreed.

"What did he do?"

X said nothing. His arm hung limply by his side. He winced when Sara moved his arm and lifted his shirt, but he did not stop her. The purplish black bruise covered most of his side.

"Oh god, Xav," Sara said. "Why do you let him do it?"

X shrugged, though the effort pained him.

"It wasn't just him," X said, his voice gentle and tame. "Tony and Jackson helped."

"The three fucking stooges," Sara said.

X laughed and Sara lit up. Binky laughed too. I was the only one who cringed.

"I'll meet you in the kitchen," Sara said. "Get some ice out. I'll put something on TV for Binky."

Sara led me through the dining room and the even larger living room, down a hallway, past a few more doors into a sunken den decorated in hunting lodge chic. X had slinked off in the other direction and was far out of earshot.

We sat down on the couch. Binky had already settled in, his consciousness winding down in preparation for the numbness brought on by TV. Sara walked over to the console, which was encased in a piece of wooden furniture the size of a dresser. She pulled the on switch and the picture expanded from a tiny dot to full screen. Sara clicked one dial around to UHF, then started the tedious process of spinning the lower one around to the right channel. The static of the empty space between stations was oddly comforting, a physical manifestation of absence. Finally, she landed on a *Leave It to Beaver* rerun.

"There, that's good," she said. "I'll just be a few minutes, then we'll head home, okay?"

We nodded. Sara leaned over and kissed the top of our head before disappearing down the long hall toward the opposite end of the house.

Big shock—the Beaver was in trouble again.

The day of my sister's funeral, my parents returned home angry—not at each other, but they had no one else to fight with.

"He had a lot of nerve showing up," my mother said.

"He loved her," my father said.

"You know what I mean," she said. "He shouldn't have been there."

"Sara would've—"

"Don't say it," my mother said, ending the fight. "Don't you fucking dare."

It was years later, when I looked at the newspaper pictures from the funeral, that I realized they were talking about X.

The world rumbled around me. At first, I thought it was an earthquake. Nothing so interesting, just a garage door opening and closing. The garage was next to the den, a door connecting them. I heard muffled voices, joking. Then they came through the door.

Anthony Righetti and Jackson Flynn. And Z.

"Who left the fucking TV on?" Z said.

"Musta been Jackson," Tony said.

"I didn't touch it," Jackson said, shrugging at the accusation, a nervous tic.

Jackson was about a foot shorter than his friends. Squat but strong. Tony Righetti, on the other hand, was large in every dimension, a solid wall.

"Fucking *Leave It to Beaver*," Tony said.

Jackson started to whistle.

"That's the Andy Griffith song, douchebag."

"Fuck you," Jackson said, with another shrug, like he didn't care when he really did.

Z held a six-pack of Budweiser, the cans tethered together by those plastic rings that choke seagulls. He was looking right at us.

That's them, isn't it?

Like children always do, Binky had been paying attention to everything I had said and thought, even while pretending not to.

Yeah, I said. *That's them.*

It was easy to see that X and Z were brothers. It was also clear that any good looks in the gene pool had made their way only to X. Everything about Z was elongated and out of proportion. Big hands and feet. Narrow shoulders and hips. His face skewed left, the eye on that side seeming larger, though I was sure it must be some sort of optical illusion. His small nose seemed to stand on the precipice of his giant mouth, ready to dive in. When he smiled at us, we were blinded by two rows of perfect, gleaming white teeth.

"Hey, kid," Z said. "What you doing on my couch?"

"I think he's watching TV," Jackson said, laughing at his own joke.

Z punched Jackson in the arm, swift and hard. Jackson grunted and retreated a step away.

"I asked the kid," Z said.

"He's so small, I didn't even see him," Tony said.

Realizing his transgression, Tony backed away from Z before he could hit him too. He held his hands up in surrender.

Z stared through us. He had two names on his mechanic's overalls—Ezekiel and Quality Motors, his dad's dealership. His presence filled the room with malice and the threat of violence.

"You don't talk?" Z said. "That's cool. We'll just watch the show then."

Z came over and sat on the couch next to us. He smelled of sweat and motor oil. Tony sat on the other side of us, significantly reducing the elevation of the couch cushions. Binky had to lean toward Z in order not to fall into Tony. Jackson perched on the edge of an ottoman off to the side.

"Who is he?" Jackson said, motioning at us.

"Must be Sara's kid brother," Z said. "That right, kid?"

Binky nodded. He stared straight ahead at the TV. I felt our little lungs expand and contract more quickly. Binky had heard my thoughts, seen what I knew, and now, surrounded by the boys who assaulted Sara, it was finally becoming real for him.

Just relax, Binky, I said. *We're okay.*

They did that to her? It really happened?

Not yet. Not yet. Just calm down.

Z freed two beers from their plastic restraints, tossing them to Jackson and Tony. The yeasty sting assaulted our nostrils as all around us the tops were popped.

"Have a beer, kid," Z said. He put a cold can in our lap, but didn't open it.

"I'd fuck June Cleaver," Jackson said. "Lookit her, just asking for it."

"You couldn't get that pussy," Tony said. "Bet Wally'd let you suck his dick though. You'd like that."

"You'd ass-ram Eddie," Jackson said.

Z laughed. I suspected that he usually laughed at his friends, rarely with them.

"June is hot, huh kid?" Z said, nudging Binky in the side. "Not like your sister, though."

"Sara is fucking hot," Tony said.

"Yeah, I'd do her," Jackson said.

"That's my brother's girlfriend," Z said sharply. Jackson slurped from his beer, chastened.

I want to go home.

Let's go find Sara, I said. *Just get up.*

But Binky couldn't move. He was rooted by the company—the fear of Z's rapid strike, the casual complicity of Tony and Jackson, the devastating reality of the unrealized future. Our breaths became more and more shallow.

I felt strangely calm, for once holding it together. Binky was panicking.

"Something wrong with him?" Jackson said. "He sounds like a sick dog or something."

"He having an asthma attack?" Tony said.

"Nah, we're cool," Z said.

He put his arm around us, pulling Binky into a gentle headlock.

That was too much for me. I had been kidding myself. Feeling Z's arm on our neck, I was overcome by panic. My tongue blew up like a balloon, cracking my palate and breaking my lower jaw. I choked on my own inability to speak.

I was in the arms of my sister's rapist.

We went pale and glassy. I'm sure of it. For a moment, the

room disappeared and we were together in the cave, curled up in fetal positions next to each other on the floor.

"Binky! What did you do to him?"

Z's arm slithered off our shoulders.

Our eyes opened. Sara stood in the doorway.

Tony moved away from me on the couch. Jackson disappeared into himself, keeping his eyes fixed on the TV.

"We didn't do nothing," Z said. "Just watching TV. Right, kid?"

Binky said nothing. We stared at Sara now, but he hadn't returned completely.

"Stay away from him," Sara said. "Come on, Binky."

When we didn't move, Sara approached the couch. She now stood in the middle of the three boys. They all watched her, hungry. I wanted to scream at her to run.

Get up, Binky, I said.

Sara held out her hand to us.

"What, I'm not good enough to hang with your brother?" Z said.

Sara turned on him, fiery eyes bathing us all in the heat of her anger. I felt Z retreat, ever so slightly, barely noticeable to anyone who wasn't sitting next to him.

"I've seen what you do to your brother," Sara said.

"Good thing he's got his nurse to take care of him," Z said, not backing down from the challenge.

Jackson and Tony started to laugh, but Sara silenced them with a withering glare.

Out of the corner of my eye, I saw X in the doorway, watching his brother.

"So I get a little rough with him sometimes," Z said. "But I can be gentle too."

Sara still held her hand outstretched to Binky. How I wished more than anything that he had already taken it.

Z grabbed her wrist, not hard, but enough.

Sara slapped him.

The universe froze. For a moment, nothing moved.

"Don't *ever* touch me, asshole," Sara said.

Then everything was motion. Binky jumped to his feet. Sara pulled him away toward X, who was shrinking back into the hall. Jackson and Tony swiveled toward Z, waiting for instructions.

And Z. Fists clenched. Jaw set. Stung by the blow. On his feet, rooted in place.

We heard him shout after us as we hurried toward the front door.

"Fucking bitch. X can't show you shit! I'll give you a real man."

X walked us to our car. He and Sara clung to each other, desperate kisses exchanged, like lovers who just escaped a burning building but weren't sure that the rest of the world wasn't also on fire.

Binky got into the front seat, but we could hear them outside.

"I'm so sorry," Sara said.

"It's okay," X said. "He deserved it."

"But now—"

"Don't worry. I'll take a walk. It'll be okay."

"I didn't—"

"Go home."

Sara got in the car next to me. The ignition turned, the engine rumbled, the tires rolled. X fell away behind us. I watched him grow smaller in the side mirror. When he knew we were safely away, he turned and walked down the sidewalk in the opposite direction, alone.

SEVENTEEN

WHEN I WAS fifteen, I went to the Spring Dance with Melissa Vorhees. We doubled with her best friend, Sharon, and Sharon's boyfriend, Jason, who was seventeen and had a car. Other kids went to what passed for fancy restaurants in our little neck of the woods. We went to the Country Kitchen in our formalwear because we thought it was ironic or anti-establishment or just funny and that made it cool. Those were days when we always thought we were in on the joke.

As we got drunk in the parking lot on swigs of tequila in Sprite bottles, our own little pre-party in the car, I realized that I was in love with Jason and not Melissa.

The rest of the evening, I caught his eye a number of times, looking for some recognition of the awkward situation we were in. While he grabbed Sharon's ass on the dance floor, while he freshened her drink from the flask in his coat pocket, while he proposed going back to his place because his parents were out of town. I always got the same look, the same smirk that says, *I think I'm getting laid tonight.*

Melissa threw up in the car and saved me from having to force myself to be sick. We took her home. She tried to kiss me, but she reeked of vomit. Sharon and Jason dropped me off next. As soon as they drove away I started to cry. The absence of him was unbearable.

Binky and I sat in the front seat of another car in another time. Sara drove slowly, checking her mirrors in the clear spots between tears. I understood exactly how she felt. She was in love. X was in a bad situation and there was little she could do to help. What she had just done had probably made it worse.

I played back what had happened over the last hour. Was it my fault? Would Sara have been there if I had not been here? I struggled with my memory to find any time that I had ever been in X's house, any time that I had ever seen a fight between Z and my sister, but I unearthed nothing. Had my presence here created the circumstances for that to happen? Would that lead to an angry Z doing what he did to my sister?

But that didn't make any sense. Because what happened to her had happened without that fight, as far as I knew. My head was again overloaded with contradictions and paradoxes.

Enough. Time to end this charade. I was not a visitor here, not a welcome guest. For two days, I had been a limited observer. That was not my purpose. I needed to take control. There was no other way. That was my task.

Sara rolled to a halt at a stop sign. She stared straight ahead out the windshield, cheeks stained with mascara tears. The streets around us were empty. There was no reason to move. Binky and I waited.

We had to do something.

I don't know what to do.

I hadn't realized Binky was paying attention to me.

You think I need to do something. I don't know what to do.

Let me help you, I said.

I don't feel very good. I want to rest.

Binky closed his eyes.

We stood before each other with a new recognition. The heaviness of what I knew now weighed on him as well. He understood that he needed to allow me access in order to get rid of me. I was a virus and he was a kid ready to take his medicine.

You go rest, I said. *I can take care of everything.*

I feel wobbly. Sick. I'll rest.

Yes, go rest, I said. *Just let me in.*

Then the car was moving, lumbering toward home. I didn't have much time. I wanted to talk to Sara before anyone else was around. I could tell her everything. I could make her understand. She would believe me.

She would be saved.

But I still didn't know how to find the voice. I could sense Binky retreating. Deep and away, to wherever he went to be alone. A closed room that only he could access, the place that scared our mother and angered our father.

A locked door.

The click echoed through the cave like a gunshot.

The door had opened.

I ran to the door I had found in the tunnel to the home of his imagination where I had been attacked by the id. It was ajar. Binky had let me in. He had ceded control.

I pushed the door open wider. I saw right through it to the passageway on the other side. Maybe I was wrong. This was nothing more than another of Binky's ineffective defenses. Just an illusion. Sleight-of-hand to prevent me from seeing what was right in front of me.

To test the theory, all I had to do was walk through the door. But I hesitated. Fusing my consciousness to Binky in this way could be irreversible. What if I became Binky? All identity of my older self lost.

The air in the tunnel changed, thickened. Binky was completely gone now, sequestered away in a secret hideout. While his absence allowed me to act, it also freed the other portions of his personality. Farther down the passageway, the cloud of flies was forming quickly.

The id flew toward me unchecked. I saw the tiny green ball of superego trailing just behind it and this time I knew that it would not help me. Binky's existence as an independent being was threatened. There was only one correct course of action for the superego in this case—destroy the intruder.

I ran through the door.

It slammed shut behind me.

And I was gone.

I GASPED.

I opened my eyes.

Binky was no longer. It was only me. There was no separation. I had appropriated the consciousness of this body. What before I could consider logically, now I could only feel. Before it had been like watching a movie. Like wearing gloves. Like hearing underwater. Now, everything was real again.

I looked around. But my brain had trouble focusing these young eyes. The zoom lens on my camera kept overshooting its mark. Blurry, focused, blurry, focused. Near, far, near, far. I closed my eyes and waited for them to stop trying to see. There was darkness, that inky pitch black I had craved before, but now it was disconcerting. My head lolled to the right, and I wasn't sure if I had moved it. Or maybe I just hadn't concentrated on keeping it upright. I lifted my head back up— it was so light—and I could not control it. I tensed my neck muscles too late and it flopped to the right. I was an infant; I needed my mother's hand to steady me.

I took a deep breath. But that too proved difficult. Too much air. I coughed. Then, I wheezed, sucking in too quickly to compensate.

This made no sense. I had lived for decades, handling these simple tasks without incident.

So I stopped trying. Just let instinct guide me. This was not an alien vessel. It was merely a different kind of car—going from an SUV to a Yugo. I had driven it before. For a long moment,

I did not move. I readjusted. Remembered how loose the gas pedal was, the give of the steering wheel, the proportions of my chassis. I reacquainted myself with my physicality, then opened my eyes again, ready to drive.

We were parked in the driveway of our house. I heard Sara turn the key in the ignition. The roar of the engines drained from my ears. The world quieted around us.

I turned my head, very slowly, very carefully, to look at my sister. Sara also took a moment with her own thoughts before speaking.

"Let's go, little man," she said. "Time to face the music."

She cranked the driver's side window up. Her hand reached for the door handle. Was I too late? We needed to be alone.

"Wait," I said.

The word bubbled up from my throat, a croak, a gargle. I sounded like I was choking. Sara looked at me with alarm.

"You okay, Bink? You gonna puke?"

I took a deep breath, meaning to calm myself. But it was too fast; it sounded like a wheeze.

"Wait," I said again. This time the voice was reedy, forced out without any depth.

We were parked halfway down the driveway. Another car I didn't recognize was parked in front of us.

"Binky, let's go in. Mom and dad are—"

"No."

Too loud. The word—throaty, gritty, deep. That one scared Sara. She put a hand on my cheek and moved me to look at her. I was grateful for the help. Her palm wandered to my forehead, checking for a fever. She was no longer crying, but her eyes were still wet. She waited for me to speak.

This was it. The moment where I changed everything.

"I…" My voice was still too morose, too possessed. I tried again, modulating upwards. "I need … to talk to … you."

My breaths came in the wrong cadence. Breaking words,

interrupting syllables. I was angry at myself for making this so hard.

Then the pounding started. Thud, thud, thud. I thought maybe it was my heart—Binky's heart—giving out.

There wasn't much time. I needed to figure out where to start.

"Don't go," I said.

Finally, the words sounded normal. I had reached a compromise between Binky's physical capabilities and my conception of voice.

"Come on, Bink," Sara said, getting impatient now that I seemed better. "I want to go inside."

"No, not now," I said. "Thursday. Don't go to the party on Thursday."

I still didn't sound right—sort of like a seven-year-old who had been smoking for three years—but she understood me now.

"Whatever you say. Let's just go inside."

She wasn't taking me seriously. Her response was the casual lying that adults do to children, assuming the kid will forget about it first. But children never forget. Not until they become adults.

"I'm serious. You have to stay home."

My tone was harsh, mature. I sounded like our father. That got her attention.

"Okay, I'll bite. Why?"

"They're going to hurt you."

Bam, bam, bam. The pounding grew louder. I understood what was happening. Someone—something—a part of me— was trying to knock down the door. They were coming for me with a battering ram. I didn't have much time.

Binky was trying to regain control.

"Stop it, Binky. That's enough. No more games."

"It's not a game," I said. The words spilled out frantically, with a hint of madness. "Z and his friends. They …"

I paused, but this was not my younger self I was talking to. I didn't need to mince words for Sara. She was old enough for the truth. But looking at her now, through Binky's eyes, she looked younger than I ever remembered her. Terrified and unsure, she was faced with me, my irrationality, and she didn't know what to do. I could see that she wanted nothing more than to turn this situation over to our parents.

"They're going to rape you. On Thursday."

BAM. Pause. *BAM*.

YOU MUST LEAVE.

The id was almost in. My time was up.

Sara was crying.

"Binky, what's going on? You're scaring me."

I felt the door being pried open. It had been splintered enough to let the id and the superego grasp at the shards and pull it apart. I could feel my grip on the consciousness slipping.

Take him away.

YOU MUST BE REMOVED.

The full out assault began. I struggled to focus on Sara, but suddenly my muscles all flinched, every neuron firing at once in opposition to the others. I felt my head jerk back and forth. My teeth chattered destructively, gnawing at my tongue, which I struggled to move.

"Mom! Dad!"

Shuddering, twitching, lurching, I found myself contained in Sara's arms. She'd scooped me up and was running toward the house. I tried to rest my head on her shoulder, but our skulls bounced off each other like billiard balls. I knew I was hurting both of us.

"Help me, please!"

The front door flew open. Through the spasms, I caught glimpses of my mother, my father. We sprinted past them inside. Ms. Mittewag's face. She must have been talking to them about my day. It was all falling apart. Giving up on control, I forced this small body to act one last time. I pressed my cheek into the side of my sister's face, my little drooling lips quivering beside her ear.

"Listen to me," I said.

That was all I managed. Then, I was gone.

I was back inside the cave, the outside world closed off to me now.

Expel him.

GET OUT.

The door was destroyed. The id, with all its talons and tentacles and rage, pulled me from Binky. Again, I was separate.

In short bursts of light, I could see the world outside twist and twirl around us. Snippets of reality. Our mother's face. Ms. Mittewag running for the phone. Our sister trying to hold our head still. Our father forcing a wooden spoon between our teeth. Someone said, we need an ambulance. Someone else begged us to talk to them. Someone else prayed between tears.

Inside, the world rumbled around us, crumbled under us. But this time the tremors didn't slow, they strengthened. They wouldn't stop. We were beyond that now. We had gone too far.

The id dismantled me. The superego hovered before me, obscuring my view of the world beyond. It directed the id toward my weakest points. The id snarled and gnashed as it tore me apart, piece by piece. The pain was excruciating and yet I was unmoved. In the distance, I saw Binky walk through the remains of the door and disappear.

The id ripped larger chunks out of me. Piles of flesh, chains of organs, latticework of bones. Soon there would be nothing.

YOU WILL LEAVE.

I panicked. I did not want to go. I didn't know if I had been successful. My task felt incomplete. I tried to fight back. The floor of the cave was littered with me. While I could move each bit individually, a tendon here, a muscle there, none of it added up to a whole. I was done. That was when I realized that there was no longer an outside world to observe.

We had blacked out. We had shut down.

Oh god, dear god, don't let us die.
GO.
Go.
Go.
I found my eyes in the corner of the cave. I closed them, covering the pupils with the palms of my severed hands, and then all was dark. I was grabbed and I was tossed away.

EIGHTEEN

"NURSE!" A FAMILIAR voice. "He's awake!"

Somewhere far in the distance, a buzzer sounded, repeatedly with no consistent rhythm. Atonal.

I felt as if I was floating out of a long dark tunnel. That noise was my siren, luring me closer, against my will.

There was a hand almost directly in front of my face; it held a small cylinder with a red button on top. Every time the thumb pushed the button, the noise outside recurred.

Groggy. So tired. Heavy.

A call button. The world smelled of plastic. There was something foreign scraping the inside of my nose, snaking down my throat. The hospital. I shifted and the bed crackled. Deeply starched and sterilized sheets.

I was me again. No longer we.

I focused on the hand. It was a struggle, but I did not give in to fatigue, the crushing desire to sleep again. The hand flowed into a hirsute forearm, a rounded bicep, a strong shoulder, a worried face. Roger.

"Hang on, someone's coming," Roger said. "Thank god."

The nurse ran into the room. She knew my name. She knew

Roger's name. She checked a machine to my left and an IV bag to my right and held my wrist for a little while, either to check my pulse or out of a vain attempt to give me comfort.

I felt like a concrete block filled with neon gas. Light and heavy. Weighed down by my own buoyancy. Insubstantially solid.

I had fallen. I suddenly remembered that. I had hurt myself. Probably full of drugs. That might explain my inability, or possibly unwillingness, to move.

No, I could move. I shifted my arm just to prove it. I had less success lifting my head off the pillow.

"Don't try to move, Benny," Roger said. "You don't have any plans."

He laughed. The nurse was gone. Like a wisp of smoke. I turned my head, looking for her or nothing in particular when I noticed three bobbleheads on the table next to my bed.

Bobbleheads?

"You like those? Picked them up from a guy outside. Only in New York do you get psychotherapy bobbleheads from a street vendor."

Again, the laugh. I soaked in it, letting it moisturize my tired, cracked skin.

"It's been two days. I … I just … I had to take a walk. Limited visiting hours. There they were. So I bought them. Thought you might find them funny."

Roger tapped each of the three figures, sending the heads careening up and down on their springs, wildly unsyncopated and dizzying. I recognized the first two—Freud and Jung in all their iconic glory. The third was a mystery. Its nameplate was obscured by one of those tiny cards that grace flower bouquets.

"Yeah, I didn't know him either. Label says it's B.F. Skinner." Roger started singing. Something about feeling angry, like a rat in a cage.

I must have looked confused.

"Sorry. Smashing Pumpkins. I'll play it for you later. When you get out of here."

I tried to ask a question, but my tongue flailed uselessly in my mouth, a bumper car with no driver.

"Easy there. Slow down. I should cut out the psych jokes, shouldn't I?"

I listed toward Roger. I focused. I spoke.

"You should."

Hoarse, the words scratched against my throat. But it was *my* voice. I wondered how long it had been since I had last talked. Seeing the tears rise in Roger's eyes, I guessed it had been awhile.

"Great," he said. "For days I've been praying you'd come back to me, and the first thing you say reminds me that you're an asshole."

Roger put one hand on my cheek as he spoke. His other hand smoothed the hair on my arm. The word "asshole" came out like a caress.

"I will miss watching that one nurse give you sponge baths though. I asked if I could get one too. I don't think he knew I was joking."

"Shut up," I said.

It was my turn to reassure. I raised my arm. After inhabiting Binky, it felt like lifting a barbell with my fingertips. Roger leaned forward to touch his lips to my palm.

"Don't ever scare me like that again," he said.

I said nothing. I didn't understand. Why was Roger here? He read my expression, just like he always could, and answered the question I hadn't asked.

"Mr. Colson called me after you fell," Roger said. He took a deep breath. "What were you doing up there?"

Roger sighed, his words trailing off. I felt his hands wrap around mine, warm and safe as a cocoon.

"I told you that stain would never come out," he said.

I laughed, though I sounded like I was choking. Roger sat

up, alarmed, so much love in that face. I didn't understand how he could be here after everything I had done, but this was what I wanted. I finally realized that. This happiness, this life. I wanted him back.

But I knew that I could not accept it unconditionally. There was a cost. I had to find out if anything had changed. It couldn't be that everything I had seen through Binky wasn't real. It had to have meant something. So, through this leaden body and this cluttered mind, I asked.

"Sara?"

Roger looked confused.

"Sarah?" he said. "The manicurist at the salon?"

"No. Sara."

My tone said more than my words. Roger softened. I knew that he did not want to bear me bad news.

"Your sister?" he said. "Oh, Ben. That was so long ago. You must remember."

I said nothing. My body quivered. I grew cold.

"After the … after what happened. This is all you told me. After that, she … killed herself."

I had left too soon. I had failed. My task incomplete. The panic rose. The cold hands wrapped around my throat. Tighter, tighter.

"My mother?"

"Do you really not remember? Why are we …"

Roger was getting frustrated. He never could hide it.

"My mother."

"She abandoned you. Your father asks you for money and treats you like shit. Can we stop now?"

All the same then. My mother, gone. My father, a pathetic shell. My sister, dead. Nothing had changed.

"I'm sorry," Roger said. "I didn't mean that. We can talk about whatever you want."

But I had my answers. I turned away from Roger.

"Hey, Benny, don't be like that."

"I'm sorry," I said.

My voice was barely a whisper. I wanted this, but I had to go back. I felt Roger's arm wrap around me. He climbed into the small bed, molding his warmth and his strength to me. This would be my anchor. This is what I would use to pull myself back from the other world. The blood pounded through my pulsing limbs. I closed my eyes.

"I have to go," I said.

"I won't let you," he said. "I'm keeping you right here."

"I love you."

I heard Roger's tears and confused them with my own. His body heaved against mine as I let go once more.

There was a chasm. A giant gaping hole in my mind. I could feel it. It rose up to meet me. It would take me back. All I had to do was let myself fall.

In the distance, above me, below me, beyond me, I heard Roger's screams—"no, no, no, help, somebody"—and then the activity growing softer and more distant, doctors and nurses grabbing my then-body and trying to revive it, snippets of dialogue—"stat," "septic shock," "clear"—followed by murky silence and contoured darkness and finally nothing at all.

NINETEEN

I OPENED MY eyes and the mist surrounded me. The world was gently opaque. Unsettling but not threatening. Just quiet. So quiet. And peaceful. So peaceful. Drifting off to sleep. Happy.

I forced myself to stand up. The tendrils of the fog parted as I rose. I could see now that they were not a single entity, but a massive collection of separate beings, each one a tendril of smoke, rolling and slithering around each other, like a school of eels clustered in a wide open sea.

They brushed against me and I felt them on my skin, sandpapery like a thousand licks from a cat's tongue. I was of interest to them; they explored the boundaries of my existence. Calculations were being made—I was being measured. But they had no eyes, no ears, no tentacles or antennae. They seemed alive, yet somehow I sensed no soul within them.

That's what scared me. Though I did not understand their purpose, I suspected they would be single-minded in pursuing it.

I was back in the cave of Binky's brain. This place had become familiar enough, so even through the veil of misty creatures, which grayed the walls further and coated my mind with a thick layer of grease, I could navigate. I took a step and they moved away, preferring to be behind me, around me, within my grasp but out of reach.

Down the passageway, I could see that the door which the id and superego had fought so hard to expel me from was wide open and unprotected.

That was when I panicked.

Binky! I said.

The eels around me flinched and squealed. They started to move faster, agitated. More of them approached me, probing, deciding. I held still and tamped down my emotions. They reacted to my call, my desperation. Calm was the only option. As I relaxed, the mist returned to its lazy state, milling around harmlessly, waiting for the next outburst. They were intruders, just as I was. We all wanted something from Binky, though I doubted our goals aligned.

Suddenly, I caught a glance of the outside world, though I couldn't tell what I was seeing. Nothing but a murky darkness. Somehow, the wall between what I saw inside and outside of Binky had eroded. I was able to discern both at once. Possibly a side effect of having been in control. Or maybe I had just adjusted to this dual reality. I didn't know why it was possible, but what was outside scared me, the nothingness of it, so I forced my focus on the internal.

Slowly, I moved into the tunnel, hoping to find Binky there. The door was a gaping hole before me, beckoning me in. I carefully sidestepped the pit, ignoring its tempting gravity, the chance to once again take control.

At the end of the passageway, the world that had been so vibrant was drained of color. Nothing moved. The mist filled the absences, occupied the space. I searched the enormity around me and found only void.

Binky, I said.

Carefully, quietly, I spoke his name. The eels closest to me paused and turned, but ultimately considered me outside the scope of their mission.

Binky, I said. *Are you here?*

We are here.

Through the mist, I saw them, the id and the superego, a mass of flesh stretched out on the ground like a speed bump, the small ball floating above it, both entities drained of color behind the undulating opacity. I walked in their direction, slowed by the eels that clustered like iron shavings around a magnet, forcing me to push through.

I did not realize how vibrant, how alive, the verdant superego had been until I saw the muddy brown ball hovering before me now.

You have returned. That was not expected.

The form at my feet, a mound of shallow breathing monster, stirred. It was covered with gray fur matted down with slick ooze. The giant rat lifted its head with a snarl, latching onto me with one vicious eye. Only then did I notice the tail, solid as a steel cable, weaving away from the grotesque into the cover of the mist. The id wanted to pounce, to rip my muscles from my bones, but the strength was not there.

Shhhh. Rest. Wait.

The superego's words were far from a comfort to me. My uneasiness spiked when I saw the hand within the pelt of the monster, tiny fingers clenched tightly around a clump of dirty fur.

Binky, I said sharply.

Shhhh.

Now, the superego was addressing me.

Don't draw them to you.

The mist closed in on me, individual tendrils poking my face with scratchy intensity.

They want us to be calm.

I could feel my emotions racing around inside my being, a hamster hopelessly spinning on a wheel. There is no room for panic. *Focus. Control.* Slowly, I moved forward to get a view over the rat, beyond the creature to the avatar of my younger self that hid behind it. There, clinging to the rodent, like a child with a steroid-pumped teddy bear, was Binky.

I forced myself to stay calm, modulating all concern from my voice, leaching my very self of emotion. Still, I asked what was on my mind. *Are we in a coma?*

The superego laughed or coughed. Some uncomfortable outburst in between.

We are drugged. We are being controlled.

Controlled. I remembered the shaking that occurred right before I'd been expelled. The seizure. They must have taken Binky to the hospital. I imagined the consultations with the doctors followed by the quick decision to treat the symptom rather than the patient. Possibly a diagnosis of epilepsy. Which would lead to the drugs. To control the seizures. To deaden the mind.

The drugs. The eels. The mist.

I looked at Binky, at myself, sadly. We did not deserve such a fate.

Why is he here? I asked.

He is hiding.

From what?

From the thing he fears.

I tamped down the urge to smack the muddy ball for the sin of cryptic smugness. But I was worried that even a casual clap might exacerbate the damage of its current state. The idea of life without a superego frightened me.

Drugs wear off, I thought. *We just need to wait.*

Then, I heard the breathing. So familiar now, but so surprising and terrifying then. The world around me reverberated with the sound—a labored, mechanical inhale-exhale, so exquisitely slow, keeping time like a maniacal metronome that signified pure evil. It was above us, outside of us, around us. Instantly recognizable—a cultural touchstone like few others.

Kohhhhh … kahhhh. Kohhhhh … kahhhhh.

Darth Vader?

I switched my focus, feeling a brief moment of joy at being able to do so. I pushed outward, past the mist, past our restrained consciousness, past my own doubt, to take a closer look at the world around us.

IT WAS DARK—THAT much I had gotten right. Not the pitch black void I had originally believed. Binky sat in a large room, sunk deep into a plush seat, feet hanging above a sticky floor. I smelled popcorn. In front of me, Darth Vader towered two stories high, reaching out his black gloved hand, manipulating the air through the power of the force to choke the living bejesus out of some hapless extra playing an Imperial functionary.

I knew that I must have seen *Star Wars* when it first came out but I didn't remember being scared. Here, in my tiny body, barely able to breathe, choked along with the actor on the screen, I wondered how I could have been anything but terrified. Relief flowed through me as Darth Vader dropped the poor bastard, and I felt Binky's consciousness retreat further inside us to wait out the remainder of the movie in a safer place. This left me alone to watch.

Glancing to the side, I saw my father sitting next to me, rapt and silent. A movie was perfect for my state. Binky, even in hiding and drugged, could not resist the popcorn tub next to us. He reached for it, clumsily, like an infant, managing to guide a greasy handful to our mouth. So, droopy and dazed, I watched *Star Wars* for the hundredth time but, for the first time, nostalgic and shell-shocked. It was my hope that by the time the movie was over, the drugs would wear off enough for us to consider our next move with a clearer head.

FOR MOST OF the ride home, my father maintained a near perfect silence. A Jedi intensity that rivaled Obi Wan. A pure Zen channeling of the Force. When he spoke, I knew that the empty space was nothing more than bitterness and jealousy.

"That was overrated," he said.

Binky turned toward our father, alarmed by the voice he heard. Lack of conviction was nothing new here, but this was something different. A despair, a resignation that chilled us.

I understood it, of course. I had been sitting there in that theater, surrounded by people experiencing the movie for the first time. Reveling in it, each one understanding that they were seeing something they had believed impossible. We had all paid witness at the birth of a phenomenon. Only I understood how fully this silly little movie would fuse with the American cultural landscape, how within a couple of years no one would believe there had ever been a world that did not contain it.

My father understood the power too, though somewhat differently. The weight of the shared experience. The joy of the crowd and the anticipation that carried through the applause during the closing credits. The need for more, the exhaustion of a story perfectly told.

The car slowed to a stop at a red light, rolling forward, threatening to drift into the empty intersection before finally coming to a stop. My father stared ahead.

"Full theater on a Thursday afternoon," he said, not to us. "Damn."

There it was. His realization that everything he worked on in that upstairs room, every word that he tapped out of that electric typewriter, would never amount to the movie he had just seen. The car was permeated with his failure, the world beyond emptier than before. The light changed. We sat for a long moment, stalled on green, considering the options. For the first time, I was thankful for the drugs Binky was on. There was no need for me to feel my father's pain. Nothing but calm.

At least the prequels will suck in thirty years, I said.

"It's okay, dad," Binky said. "The prequels will suck."

Our father laughed. "I think you mean sequels, buddy."

I felt Binky smile a broad, stoned grin. We drove toward

home. He had emerged from his hiding place and I found myself aglow in his presence.

Until I thought through what my father had said.

Thursday. Today is Thursday.

Throughout my life, doctors had given me many different drugs to try and manage my condition. I considered what I understood about how different classes of narcotics affect the human mind. It was not a mysterious process. It was not a mist clouding over an ethereal consciousness. It was nuts and bolts—a physical reaction to a changing environment within the architecture of the brain. Receptors blocked, glands stimulated, natural defenses alerted or muted. It was science, not alchemy.

Yet, here I was, an interloper. Not part of the structure, merely a parasite within it. I should have been immune to the real, the concrete, the external world. The drugs should not have affected my unmoored consciousness. They should not have dulled my senses and allowed me to enjoy a thirty year old movie I had seen dozens of times. I should not have been caused to forget so easily the reason I leapt back into the void to get here, away from Roger, away from me.

And yet I did.

Today was Thursday.

The day it happened.

We floated toward that cursed house. My father glided the car into the garage as smoothly as a Tie Fighter onto an Imperial Cruiser. There was still a residual happiness in his expression, remembering what Binky had said, considering the possibility that what he had just seen was just a house of cards that would fall apart with the crappy prequels, unaware that that would only happen in a galaxy far far away, a few billion dollars into the future.

"Come on," our father said. "Dinner time."

Binky did not move. I did not want him to. We both understood that if our sister was not in the house that there would be little left to do but wait until she returned home with the cops in a few hours, a broken shell. I felt my father's hand on our shoulder.

"Those pills are some real downers, huh?" he said. "Look, it's just temporary. Until we can figure out what to do. Just stay with me, okay?"

Binky and his father looked through each other. It was all they could do.

THE HOUSE WAS silent. The dread rose within us—the doubt, the regret. What if Sara had already gone? I was plotting out how Binky and I would get out of the house, how a seven-year-old could get to that park at night, hoping that Binky would have the courage to take us where we needed to go, when the three of us—Binky, our father and me—walked into the dining room. There, congealed in rage and sadness, my mother and my sister sat across the table from each other, untouched plates of food before them. Charles was there too, eating blissfully, happy to have a front row seat at the fight. I could tell that they had worn each other out screaming—they were both still flushed.

Everyone turned toward us.

"Where have you been?" my mother said.

"*Star Wars*," my father said. "What's for dinner?"

It was a stupid question, of course. We could all see the meatloaf and iceberg lettuce salad on the table. Binky was starving. I felt it too. The popcorn hadn't been enough. That medication had left us unsatisfied, empty. My father took his seat at the head of the table and we walked around to ours. Sara and our mother stared at our father. We all waited.

"Looks great," he said. "Let's eat."

Charles and Binky exchanged looks. He stared at us with the same languid hatred as always. It dawned on me that he would be pissed that we'd seen *Star Wars* without him. Binky smiled and Charles speared an innocent cherry tomato.

"How was everyone's day?" my father asked.

He was not a stupid man. The question was a provocation. A gauntlet thrown at my mother. A dare for her to try and draw him into whatever maternal concern he wasn't interested in today. She took something out of her pocket and tossed her own challenge onto the table.

"Look what I found in your daughter's room."

The condom package landed next to the cruet of salad dressing. It was so round and bright in its plain cellophane wrapper. Like a poisoned Halloween treat. Like a candy-colored landmine.

Wisely, my father avoided getting too close to it, choosing instead to plop a chunk of meat onto his dish as he gathered his thoughts.

My mother pre-empted him.

"She's grounded."

Binky stared at the condom. I could feel that he knew that it was important, although he didn't know why.

What is that?

A condom, I said.

We were well past the point where I would do anything but tell him the truth.

What's it for?

It helps keep you from getting pregnant when you have sex. You put it on your penis to catch the sperm.

Binky fell silent.

Our mother had returned her attention to Sara, eyes boring through her, trying to convey a message that she knew had already failed. Sara was a black hole, defiantly snuffing out all emotion and light.

So I wasn't completely honest with Binky. I understood the significance of that condom more than anyone else in the room. I knew what the night meant to Sara, how she had decided to give herself to X. I also knew the defense lawyers at her rape trial would use the presence of a condom in her purse as evidence that she was a girl of questionable morals. But it was my mother's reaction to that condom that struck me. Though I resided in Binky's head, I might as well have been a guest in hers. That veneer of indignant anger was thin and fragile, barely masking the hurt and fear of seeing the tragedy of her own decisions repeated in her daughter. She knew the consequences of making the choice that Sara was about to make.

My mother had three children, and two of us were mistakes. Sara, of course, started it all. She was the stupid mistake, the result of the carelessness of my parents that started the daisy chain of events that had landed us at this table on that night. I, on the other hand, was the honest mistake. The unfortunate consequence of a night of rekindled passion more than a decade after the fires had been extinguished, resulting in an extension of both of their sentences. Only Charles was planned—neither my father or mother wanted to raise an only child—and he was the one they ignored.

Our gentle suburban tragedy.

"I have a date tonight," Sara said.

"You're not going anywhere," our mother said.

They both turned to our father. He picked up his napkin and dabbed the corner of his mouth.

"Can we discuss this later?" he said. "I'm starving."

He might as well have slapped my mother. It would have hurt her less. Sara smiled daggers.

The range of ways that people can damage each other astounded me. But before that dinner I had not attributed this motivation to my own family quite so clearly. I finally saw how much of a struggle it had always been for both of my parents to raise us. It did not come naturally to them. Either of them would have had trouble with the selflessness of this task on their own, but working in concert was a near impossibility. They took the loss of self as a personal affront hoisted upon them by the other. Every moment an unforgivable slight that required payment of a pound of flesh.

In the silence that followed, food was passed around the table. Binky filled our plate and started to eat. To him, this confrontation was over. The tension was a constant; it was the eruptions that bothered him. But the drama was not over. Our mother had a final play.

"I have inventory at the store tonight," she said.

No one responded. It did not seem at first like a question.

"Given Binky's condition, someone needs to be responsible for him while I'm gone."

Now she had everyone's attention. I felt our heart rate quicken. Binky did not like being a pawn, though he would not have described it that way.

"Charles can do it," Sara said quickly. "He's not doing anything."

"I might be," Charles said.

His protest was ignored. My sister had made a classic mistake, her parry opening her up on two fronts.

"Your father will be writing while I'm at the store," our mother said. "Sara, you need to take care of Binky."

Our father nodded, saying nothing. Sara had lost.

I could feel her gearing up to continue the fight, but then she looked at us and her will dissolved. I knew Binky's hangdog look could not be ignored. In that moment, I felt as if maybe this night would pass uneventfully, the horrors of the past, of the near future, averted at last.

We have to stay with her all night, I said to Binky. *Make sure she doesn't leave the house.*

Binky said nothing. He just dipped a cucumber in Ranch dressing and took a bite. As the crunch and tang of it infused our consciousness, we basked anew in the pleasing warmth that Sara brought us.

DON'T TAKE IT, I said.
She said I have to.

You don't have to do everything adults tell you, I said.

Our mother kneeled in front of us. We were in the kitchen. In one hand, she held a plastic cup of apple juice; in the other, palm up, a small pinkish pill.

"Come on, Binky," she said. "I've got to go. Two gulps and it's gone."

I had sneaked a look at the prescription bottle while she was pouring the juice.

Luminal. Phenobarbital. Some serious shit.

No wonder we'd been so zoned out.

How can I not take it?

Tuck it under your tongue, I said. *Then swallow some juice. Spit it out when she's not looking.*

A roadmap to deceit. I couldn't make it any simpler. I could feel Binky hesitate. The transfer was made from our mother to our tiny hands. We considered the pill clamped between our thumb and forefinger. The cup cold and wet in our other hand.

Binky, don't, I said.

"Binky, please," she said.

You're an adult too.

No, no, I'm you, I said.

It was too late. Binky had made up his mind. He tossed the pill to the back of his throat and it was gone even before the juice sloshed around behind it. I've always been able to take a pill, with water or without, two or three at a time, one of my hidden talents.

Our mother hugged us, tightly, with a sense of remorse. Through Binky I felt her breathe and wondered if she was about to cry.

"I'll see you in the morning. I'm sorry … but I have to go."

Binky clung tight, devouring her.

It'll be okay, I told myself. Sara is upstairs, grounded. By morning, this will all be over.

I want it to be over.

You shouldn't have taken the pill, I said.

We stood on the stairs and watched our mother latch the door carefully behind her, making barely a click.

I wanted to take it.

Why? I said.

But I already knew.

When I took the pill, you went away and I was happy. I want to be happy.

I don't know if I said it or thought it or dreamed it, but somehow it was there.

I wanted to be happy too.

TWENTY

UPSTAIRS, EVERY DOOR was closed. No lights on. It was dark and cold. We were alone. So much for someone keeping an eye on us. We were tired. A bit woozy, a bit dizzy. We were having trouble remembering where we were or how we got there. Our day could have easily come to an abrupt end right there, in the middle of the hallway, a luxurious nap deep in the folds of the shag carpet.

Instead, we knocked on Sara's door. But it wasn't Sara's room. We were turned around in the hallway, confused. Charles opened the door and pulled us into his room. He smelled funny. As if he'd soaked for three days in a vat of Old Spice. Now, far too late to expel the Luminal, we were nauseated. It didn't help that he grabbed our shirt and pushed us up against the wall.

"You little shit," Charles said. "I've been waiting to get you alone."

I didn't know what he was talking about and I could tell that Binky didn't either. It didn't really matter. We didn't care. We felt loose and light.

"You told them I told you all that sex stuff you were saying at school," he said.

"I didn't say that," Binky lied.

Our voice wasn't scared. I could see in Charles' face that Binky's reaction freaked him out. He was so calm. It might have been the Luminal, but he wasn't sure. The doubt lined his forehead. He knew that even a scrawny kid like Binky sensed no danger around him. Charles' hands shook as he held us there. The sweat from his hands soaked through our T-shirt.

I realized that I had never asked him how he felt when our mother disappeared. We'd never talked about Sara's rape. I had ignored him, just as my parents had. I, too, was guilty.

"Don't do it again," he said.

In one last assertion of control, he slammed us into the wall. It hurt, but only a little. Charles let us go. We struggled to find solid footing on the undulating floor. Our brother grabbed his backpack. It all seemed wrong. He was leaving the room—we were staying.

"I'm going out," Charles said. "Don't tell Dad."

Every move he made, the gestures, the expressions, everything, told us that he wanted us to tattle on him. But I knew Binky wouldn't. I remembered not thinking much about my brother when we were growing up. Now, I wanted to stop him, to let him know that I didn't think he was irrelevant.

Instead, we let him go. As Charles stomped off, I thought of Sara in the room across the hall. I considered her bedroom window to be her path to the outside world. Somewhere in the distance, the front door opened and closed; Charles was gone.

Back out in the hallway, we took extra care to ensure we found the right door to Sara's room.

She has to be in there, right?

Right, I said.

Because if she isn't—

She is, I said. *She has to be.*

I don't know how long we stood there outside our sister's

door. Time was lost to us. We might have fallen asleep, but that seems unlikely. A reverie, perhaps. A departure into another world where neither Binky nor I had ever been, somewhere where we stood on equal footing. A place of dark and silence and stasis. Sara opened the door and brought us back. The light from her room flooded the hallway, bathing us in its relief.

"Damn, Bink, you scared the hell out of me," Sara said. "How long have you been standing there?"

"I don't know."

"Hey, little man, you feeling okay?"

We nodded. Our eyelids drooped. Sara put a bare arm around our shoulders. She held us up and led us down the hall.

"Let's get you to bed."

The spangled top she wore left her back bare, not that it covered up much of her front either. The tiny disks that covered the fabric glinted in the weak light, blinding me. The garment was a remnant of disco that would soon become passé then ironic then cool again in twenty years or so when my friends took me to the clubs where I felt awkward and uncomfortable and fully aware that the women wearing that kind of top knew I was gay.

So familiar, that top.

So familiar.

Drifting off into a memory, Binky by my side.

That top. The spangled top. Ripped. Sticking out like confetti from under a scratchy police-issue blanket.

The top she wore the night she was raped.

She's going out, I said.

I'm so tired.

You can't let her leave.

I felt my words disappear into a well full of molasses.

"Man, you're getting heavy," she said.

Sara was carrying us to our room, short quick steps, in a hurry to be safely rid of us. She had a date.

Binky, listen to me, I said.

Leave me alone.

This is it. Right now. If you don't stop her, they'll do horrible things to her.

Shut up.

His argument seemed perfectly reasonable. I wanted to stop talking, stop thinking, as Sara laid us down on the bed, pulling the covers up to our shoulders. She had not bothered to undress us, to put us in pajamas, such was her haste. I could feel Binky pushing her away, even as he embraced her and accepted her lips on his cheek. He was ready to be discarded.

It cannot end this way.

Go to sleep.

Sara sang us a lullaby. That song we loved. The one I thought I only knew from my mother's voice that I now realize was owned by Sara.

The Sara we knew. The Sara I forgot. The Sara who was standing up. The Sara who was walking toward our bedroom door. The Sara who was whispering for us to have sweet dreams. The Sara who was disappearing.

The Sara we were about to lose forever.

"No!"

Our voice. Reedy and nasal and young and strong. Desperate. Piercing.

"Don't leave me!"

"Binky, shhhhhh," she said, hurrying back into the room.

We got louder. We were going to succeed.

"You can't go!"

We were again in her arms. I could feel her anger, not at us but at the world. Her caress was gentle. She held us to her chest, smothering the outburst. The spangles scratched our face and our tears coated them.

"Don't!"

A shadow appeared in our doorway. Our father stood there, forced to action by Binky's screams.

"What's going on?" he said.

"Nothing. I'm just putting Binky to sleep."

Sara spoke to us.

"Hush now, little man. That's enough. Get some rest."

Binky let the waves wash over him. We fell back hard onto the soft pillow. It accepted us. They were in the doorway, our dad and Sara, tense shadows. We watched them for a moment.

"Are you going somewhere?" our father said.

"I'm going out."

Our eyes closed. It could not be helped. The fighting was over.

"You can't stop me," Sara said.

A long, empty space. A decision. An admission.

"Fine. Do whatever you want."

My father was letting her go. It made no one happy. Sara did not squeal with glee or thank him with a girlish twang of Daddy-loves-me victory. He simply decided not to care and she decided to accept that.

I wondered if all the anger and spite that had consumed him the rest of his life had taken root in that moment. By refusing to be Sara's parent, by refusing to be our mother's husband, by refusing to be better than he was, he had condemned his daughter. He must have realized that. He must have known.

That was his regret. His sin.

Binky was gone now, having fully succumbed to the Luminal. I tried to maintain a link to the outside world even after Binky's eyelids rolled down, plunging us back into the darkness of our cave. I, alone, was conscious. I heard my father and sister walk away from each other, taking different paths down the hallway, into their own unfortunate futures.

I turned inward—I had nowhere else to go—to try and determine if this was the way it had to end.

TWENTY-ONE

THE MIST WAS heavy. It bore into me, down on me. I struggled to move. Binky was gone and I was left in a dark place, wet and sticky, as if I'd been rolled into a ball of cotton candy. It could not end like this. I could not let myself sleep, peacefully unaware, until we would wake to the sound of the doorbell and the two police officers bringing Sara home in tatters.

We could just lie here in bed. Warm, soft, comfortable. We could stay here forever.

The mist cocooned me, grabbed me tight and held me down on the floor of the cave. Its caress promised change. *Don't worry. When you wake up, you will be transformed into something new, a complete metamorphosis.* When I flexed, it contracted. I was being strangled. Soon, I would be permanently motionless and all would be lost. I screamed. There was no sound. The filaments snaked into my ears, my nose, my mouth, shutting out the world within.

I made out a large shape through the mist. The hairy mass of the id on the floor nearby. It bristled back, heaving steadily with sixteenth-note breaths. Long claws extended fully out of its calloused paws, pointed in my direction, as if it had been coming for me when something else felled it. The mist covered the monster like a blanket of fresh snow. It was beaten but not dead.

They are killing us, I said.

The id did not stir. I wondered if I was too late.

They are killing him, I said. *They are killing you.*

The massive hindquarters of the animal flinched, like a dog running in its sleep.

I WILL SLEEP.

You will die, I said.

The mist swirled around us, water coming to a boil.

I WILL DIE?

Yes, I said. *It is killing you. Trust me.*

My last statement took it too far. Of course, this elemental creature, this segment of my young mind, did not trust me. I was fundamentally untrustworthy, *that* it knew. But it felt trapped, oppressed, and it considered my words. Somewhere my younger self was blissfully ensconced within the calm of the Luminal, tucked in tight with its superego cradled in its arms. But here, our basest instincts sensed that something had been taken from it. I played on its innocence and fear. The id struggled to its feet. It was no longer the giant rat, but a creature much larger, a formless golem. It loomed over me, filling the chamber with its bulk. The mist that held it down snapped away, useless Lilliputian ropes on Gulliver.

YOU DID THIS.

I had woken the beast. Now, I needed to manipulate it. The mist was solidifying around us, strengthening for an attack on whichever one of us seemed the most agitated. I needed the id to play that role.

Yes, I said. *I want to kill you.*

Both the id and the mist were faster than I expected. The monster lunged for me, a mass of fangs, claws and spikes. Then it disappeared. I heard it thrash within the thick ball of

Luminal yarn. The air elsewhere in the room had thinned, allowing me a clear view to the passageway where the door was. I ran for it as the chaos behind me faded from a snarl to a whimper to nothing.

The door was still open, but the mist had wrapped around it, creating a barrier of spun silk. I crashed into the spider webs, expecting to tear through easily. Instead, I stuck there, held tight by the viscous strands, thicker than I expected. I wriggled my fingers through to the other side. I could sense that the mist understood my subterfuge. Soon, I too would be surrounded and subdued. I flailed, clawing through the barrier with my nails, my elbows, my teeth. I was the monster, the unbridled aggregation of self-interest. I was here to save her. My task. I could not fail. I would not fail. Everything that I had ever turned my back on. All of the selfish moments when I refused to give myself to others. The anger at my parents. The neglect of Charles. The pain I'd caused Roger. The unnamed child, abandoned in Guatemala, my daughter. All of it hinged on this moment. I needed to break through to the other side so that everything would change.

The mist came for me. I felt the wall give. I tumbled through the door, into Binky's motor cortex. I took control once again.

TWENTY-TWO

WE WERE STILL in bed. I opened our eyes.

It was easier this time, less disorienting. I was far more comfortable, literally slipping into my own skin. I had no problems controlling my younger self's actions this time. I became me, without a hitch.

When I stood up, our limbs felt coated with a thin laminate, barely present but nonetheless heavier. I wondered if this was the drugs or if it was merely the beginning of an inevitable and lengthy aging process. The hallway was still dark. A sliver of light escaped from the crack beneath my father's office door. I considered and rejected making an appeal to him. His track record was clear. He did not realize that Charles was gone, did not care that Sara was. Best case scenario, my father would walk us down the hall and put us back to bed; worst case, he'd just tell us to leave him alone. It saddened me to realize that I believed there was no possibility he would listen to what his sedated seven-year-old son had to say, no matter how distraught and desperate the entreaty.

Standing in my childhood hallway, alone in the dark, I wanted Roger more than ever. I wanted him to see what I saw, to feel what I felt. Maybe it would be best if he was there as his own seven-year-old self, so that we could be friends— not lovers, not adults, not complicated beings weighed down by our own history and doubt. I wanted him to understand the man down the hall and behind the door. Then, he would know why I was terrified of repeating my father's mistakes, of showing a child his indifference. I wanted him to feel the absence of my mother the way I felt it.

Sometimes, when I walled off my feelings or refused to engage with someone I cared about, I felt my parents' genes there within me, grinding away like tiny robots on an assembly line, forming me into a perfect replica of their imperfect selves. How could I—so fatally flawed—adopt a child? That was what I had always wanted to say to Roger, but never had. How could I risk doing to a child what had been done to me? Particularly a child who had already been abandoned by one set of parents. How could I, in good conscience, subject that girl to a lifetime with a father who might abandon her again?

I wanted Roger there at that moment, to tell him finally why I had rejected that child, to say what I should have said when we started fighting, before I pushed him out the door, before he left. Before I abandoned him. I know what he would have done—he would have taken me in his arms and told me that the fear of being indifferent is not the same as indifference itself.

And I would meet him at the airport and I would get on that plane with him and we would find our daughter and we would bring her home together.

That's what I was thinking about as I walked down the stairs and out the front door, into the warm night, alone.

I don't know when I started running, but I knew where I was going. The bookstore was about a mile from the house. I had walked that route a million times as a kid, as a teenager, with my mom and without her. But now I was running. It felt good, liberating, not a trot but a full-out sprint. I wondered how long

I could sustain it. Quite a long time as it turned out. Nothing tethered me but my own thoughts.

Binky's youth was accommodating indeed. I flung myself down streets, skidding around corners, barely avoiding street signs and lampposts, occasionally tumbling headlong onto someone's lawn, only to bounce back to my feet and continue on without breaking stride. I was strong; I was invincible.

I had a plan. Our mother would listen to us. I knew she would. Her seven-year-old Binky leaving home in the middle of the night with a prophesy about her only daughter would be undeniable. We—the three of us—would save Sara.

There was temptation, old instincts rearing up, inevitable. Running with this abandon led to thoughts of escape, from my family, from my future, from the rape, from everything that had shaped me and ruined me. I could run forever, away from here, directly into a new life, independent of all that came before and after.

The headlights of a passing car blinded me momentarily. I ran through them, and then we were next to each other, me on the sidewalk, the car driving down the street in the opposite direction. The driver was a middle-aged man, stooped and bald, probably counting the days until he could eject his children from the house and send them off to some college or vocation. We locked eyes for a moment, neither of us moving as fast as we thought we were. I could see him thinking that he should stop and ask why a young boy was running down the street at night, alone. Then I was gone and he was gone and I knew without a doubt that I was still trapped and alone and in need of help.

I turned the last corner, emerging into what passed for downtown. There was a light on in the diner and a couple of loners sitting at the window tables, but otherwise everyone had gone home for the evening. The bookstore was also dark, though as I approached I could see lights on in back. I stopped in the alcove, under the Purgatorio sign, and struggled to catch my breath. It took longer than I expected. I almost lay down right there in the doorway. My wind recovered, I opened the door. The little toy bell tinkled over my head. I knew that my mother would not hear it in the back. The sound of it renewed the urgency of my mission. We walked straight toward the light in the back office.

I should not have been surprised. There are things that I should have noticed over the years, so many things I chose to ignore. Binky stirred within us, sensing the moment perhaps. We stopped behind a low rack of books to be shelved. There, with our eyes just peering over the hardcover spines, we saw him.

Conrad was even skinnier than I expected, all sinew and Iggy Pop physique. His shirt was off. But even that could be explained away. It was a hot night, but still too early in the summer to turn on the air conditioning. He picked up a book, made a mark in a ledger and set it aside.

All was routine here. The only thing out of place was us.

I felt Binky shifting nervously. He sensed my hesitation. Our tiny body tensed.

I didn't want to talk to Conrad. I wanted our mother.

She appeared in the doorway, crossing the room directly behind him. My mother was fully clothed, and somehow that made what followed worse. She paused. There was plenty of room to pass by. She did not need to touch him. But her hand reached out, second nature, finding his hair, wrapping the strands around her fingers. Her palm wandered gently down his back, tracing the outlines of a shoulder blade and the ridges of his spine, before coming to a rest on the waistband of his jeans. She gave a playful tug on his belt. Conrad glanced over his shoulder, a hint of a smile—*later*, it promised—and he returned to counting books. She continued to the other side of the office, out of our sight, leaving us with only Conrad to look at once again.

We ran again. Just turned and headed back for the door as

quickly as we could go. Still a bit unsteady and tired from our previous sprinting, I know that we knocked things over, books, displays. We made a lot of noise. Our mother heard us. Conrad heard us. We hit the door hard, sending the little bell jangling, grating and angry this time. I don't know if they saw us. I just know they didn't catch us.

As we ran, I thought about Conrad, the strange quiet man who always talked to me when I came into the store. In my teenage years, I suspected at times that he was hitting on me, offering suggestions on books, asking about what I was studying, but I had been wrong. He took an interest in me because he knew me better than I suspected. He experienced my life through my mother. All those years, she must have talked to him about me and my brother and our father and her life and her despair.

We slowed and entered a playground. There, we found a bench and collapsed while I continued to spin out.

Did the affair continue after the rape? It must have. Looking back now, it is clear to me that my mother had someone, though she hid him from us expertly and in plain sight. My father must have known. Maybe he didn't care.

Her disappearance after dropping me off at college suddenly made sense. I could now impose a logical overlay on top of the history. Conrad had been waiting for her for a dozen years, patiently, screwing her on the side in earnest and in shadow, knowing that as soon as the last of her children was gone, she would run off with him. That's what had happened. He was waiting for her at a rest stop off I-95 that day, the end and the beginning of a long-simmering romance, a happy ending for an unrequited love fully consummated after a decade of deceit and tragedy. Maybe that's how it was. Maybe not.

One thing was certain to me then. My mother's undying regret—the feeling that consumed her whenever she passed through the front door of our cursed house—was that she decided to go be with Conrad that night rather than staying home to make sure Sara didn't go out.

The playground equipment resembled giant sleeping monsters in the poorly lit park. It amazed me that children were allowed to play on this equipment, all metal and rust. Without modern spring restraints, the seesaws could drop from great heights, jarring the life out of small riders and crushing little fingers and toes. The roundabout could spin at dizzying speeds until one or more kids flew off at Mach 5. Climbing bridges had no guardrails and slides were too steep. Even the Earth below it all was dangerous: hard, unforgiving concrete. This is the world in which Binky lived, in which I grew up—clearly no one was paying attention.

Our eyes closed. We had stretched out on the bench.

You can't sleep, Binky said.

His voice inside our head felt like cashmere being rubbed on the roof of our mouth. The world remained black. Our breathing evened out. Dreams approached.

Wake up! Binky screamed.

I found him in the cave. Binky looked smaller than before, less substantial. I was different as well. I was more than just me—I was the walls, the floor, the essence of the cave, looking at him from every angle at once.

Why?

I asked the question. I struggled to find the reason. I was tired. Sleeping here in the park seemed like a pretty good idea. Just to sleep and dream and not care.

We have to help Sara, Binky said.

He was so small, so helpless, pleading with me. I was everything. I was all-powerful. Then, I understood. Fleeing from the bookstore, I had assumed that Binky had regained control. I didn't remember being expelled, but it didn't make sense to me that I would run. Binky was the child; he would run. But, of course, that wasn't true. I was still in control. It was me who had brought us to this park, who wanted to go to sleep, who wanted to avoid what must be done. I spoke with Binky's voice and he used mine.

You don't know what it was like.

Tell me, Binky said.

Binky listened. I opened our eyes and rolled onto our back. Together, we stared up at the stars and the wisps of clouds weaving among them.

In the morning, no one will talk. Mom and Dad will pretend to be normal, but you'll know. Sara won't come out of her room. Even when you knock, she won't let you in. Even when you plead. You will beg, you will cry. She won't answer. She just won't open it. You'll think it will change. But the silence lasts for days, then weeks, then months. People will stop talking whenever you enter the room. You will be alone.

I don't want to be alone, Binky said.

I'm not sure we have a choice. I'm not sure we can do anything.

We can save Sara, Binky said.

How can you be sure? What if everything I remember is wrong?

That was going to be it. My final words. It was too hard, too tiring. We would sleep. Right here. In the middle of nowhere. Forever.

I know for both of us, Binky said.

Then, he was there with me. In control together. Truly sharing governance of this body of ours. I felt him standing by my side and I knelt to pick him up. Lifting Binky in my arms, I held him tight, threatening to strangle us both. His little arms crushed the life into me. We clung to each other, knowing no other way. Our toothpick legs swung to the ground and our pipe cleaner arms pushed us up off the bench. We started to walk.

TWENTY-THREE

W<small>E STOOD AT</small> the edge of the parking lot near the Grove. In the distance, we could see the Shelter at the top of the best sledding hill in town, looming there like the house in *Psycho* past the sea of soccer fields and baseball diamonds. The very sight of it sickened us. A couple of years after Sara's rape, people started to hold parties up there again, on the second floor with the view, despite its history, some because they didn't know what had happened, others because it was the only place in town that offered a decent view. The parties were family affairs, corporate retreats, picnics the day after a wedding, potlucks the night before a conference. Sometimes, in high school, I'd park in the lower lot to see if anyone was in the Shelter. When I found a party, I'd fire up a joint and stare at the demonic building and its temporary hell-bound inhabitants, so far away, trying to reflect the fire in my eyes through the tinted windshield, focusing a deadly laser ray. I wanted the place to burn down—I wanted the people inside to burn with it.

We forget. We suppress. We move on.

As with every party in the Grove, we could hear it before

we saw it. As we got closer, coming around that last thicket of bushes, we could smell it—stale beer and sweet smoke. The Grove was a collection of a half dozen picnic tables surrounded by trees, out of sight. Shortly after Sara's rape, the cops would break up the parties pretty quick, but by the time I was in high school, they had again become lax in their enforcement. The Grove seemed a place out of time. It was not close enough to any houses to attract a noise complaint. You could almost convince yourself you were camping, out in the wilderness, starry sky above, a place where no one got hurt, where nothing bad could ever happen. A place to drink and smoke pot and be invincible.

We were scared. But there was no time for that. We each had our panic, the combined force of which could have incapacitated us. But the task was so clear. So we walked into the thicket with a determination we had not felt previously, a newfound resolve. We hoped against hope that Sara was still down here.

The Grove was bigger than I remembered and the party was smaller than expected. Only about twenty kids milled around, about a football field away from us. We recognized the outline of the lonely figure sitting on a solitary picnic table close by. It was Charles. He had come to the party, but he couldn't bring himself to join it.

When he saw us approaching, he didn't seem the least bit surprised. Relieved, maybe. Happy to have someone to talk to, to have something to do.

"Mom's gonna kill you," Charles said.

We nodded, like there was nothing more natural in 1977 than a seven-year-old wandering around in the dead of night. We took a seat on the table next to our brother. There, in the glow of the clear night, we could see his haunted expression. Paler than usual. Lost.

"We need to find Sara," we said.

"Sara," Charles said.

He played with the word on his tongue, as if it was a foreign concept, a lovely remnant from a distant time.

"Is she over there?" we asked.

"Sara," he said again, this time soaked in regret. "They took her."

Charles didn't move. He stared across the great expanse of the Grove at his classmates. Our brother, conflicted and frozen. We wanted to hit him, but we put a hand on his shoulder instead.

"When I got here, she wasn't here yet. She showed up later, but she didn't see me. She was with her friends. She could barely walk straight. They must've been drinking for a while already. She didn't see me."

He seemed to realize that he'd already said that last part. Charles ran his hand over the wood of the picnic table, feeling the years of crusted-on food and beer under his fingertips. He wanted something from us—absolution, perhaps.

We spoke to ourselves. Our voices. Discussing.

We don't have time for this.

Wait. This is important.

Charles' story continued to flow freely from him.

"I watched for a while longer. I thought about going home. But I didn't move. She did what she does, I guess. Talked to some friends. Flirted with some guys. Smoked some pot. You know how Sara is."

It seemed wistful, the way he talked about Sara, like she was already gone. That's what he was trying to tell us.

"Then, X showed up. They talked for a while. He led her away from the party toward the parking lot. That's when she saw me. I didn't say anything. She just kind of sneered at me. You know. Sara."

We reeled. If she'd gone with X, then maybe everything was okay. Maybe they'd left the party together. Maybe X knew what his brother had planned and was protecting Sara. But that's not what Charles' face betrayed. He was trying not to cry.

"I was really going to leave then. I was mad. She doesn't always have to be a bitch to me." Again, he stopped. Charles looked chastised, like he was speaking ill of the dead. "I mean, well, you know. I'm sorry."

I don't understand. Is Sara okay?

I don't know.

"I heard a scream. Sara shouting, angry. I ran to the parking lot. Z and two other guys were pulling her into their car. It happened so fast. Then, they were gone. I didn't do anything."

"What about X?"

"He went with them."

We stared at Charles. Charles watched the party, paralyzed.

"We know where they went," we said.

"I didn't do anything."

"We have to help Sara."

"Why couldn't she have been nice to me?"

"Charlie—"

"No one else helped her. I don't even know if they heard her."

"We have to help her."

"I can't—"

"You have to. You're her brother. You're our brother. You have to."

It was simple and true. Charles turned toward us and we smiled.

"How do you know where she is?"

"We just know."

Charles paused, studying our face carefully.

"You okay, Bink?"

"We know she's in the shelter. We still have time."

"Why do you keep saying 'we'?"

We tried to separate out the two parts of our self, struggling to form words that could explain our situation.

"We are we." Of course, it came out wrong. "It is me and me. Me from now. And me from the future. We're together."

We looked into the face of my brother and for the first time the disdain was gone, replaced by unfettered concern. He did love us, at his core, beyond the horrors of his freshman year, before the nightmare of our life to come. This was a time, fleeting but possible, when we might have become friends.

"You from the future? Where is he?"

"He is with me always," we said. "We."

It sounded even crazier in our tiny reedy voice. But Charles did something that no one else could have done. Only our brother, with all of his sci-fi desire and technological ardor. He was truly the only person in our family who maintained a sense of wonder, and therefore an openness to the possibility of the impossible.

"So that's how you know what's going to happen to Sara, isn't it? He's telling you." Charles paused. "You're telling yourself?"

We nodded. We cried, hot salty tears thawing out our fear. Charles hugged us, a completely selfless act beyond his years.

"Let's go then," he said. "We still have time."

Together, we ran across the fields and up the hill.

TWENTY-FOUR

THE SHELTER TOWERED above us, this evil place cutting inky shards out of the cloudless night. We couldn't breathe—we didn't want to. What if we were too late? The thought of walking in on our sister already broken and bruised proved too much for us. We were overwhelmed by the image of us standing in the doorway, watching them finish, powerless to do anything but cry with her.

"You're sure she's in there?" Charles said.

"Yes."

Our voice was suddenly very far away. We had become encased in ice, frozen by our own fear.

"What are we waiting for?"

"We can't move," we said.

"You're not having another seizure, are you? Mom and Dad'll kill me."

That was what he thought about. Everyone being angry at him. We realized that maybe he didn't believe us. Maybe he just went up to the Shelter, expecting to find it empty, in order to make it easier to take us home. We did not want to go in. We couldn't face the possibility that our loss was unavoidable.

"Let's go," Charles said.

In a single confident motion, he slung us up onto his back. As we reached around his neck to hold on, he jostled us forward to the entrance of the Shelter. Charles was stronger than we expected, bearing our weight easily. We went inside together.

Whoever designed the Shelter put the staircase to the second floor in the dead center of the giant room. No, it wasn't really a room—more like a loft with no walls. Railings demarcated the space between outside and inside, barely high enough to keep people from falling one story to the parking lot below—that happened every couple of years. There wasn't much to keep you from falling down the stairs in the center of the room either. That happened about once a summer. The entire place was an accident waiting to happen.

We ascended, carried by Charles, to the second floor. Then, we saw them. Someone had already ripped Sara's top off. She cowered in the corner, holding the shreds of it over her breasts. Her skirt bunched up around her thighs, revealing every muscle in her tensed legs.

You were right. They hurt her.

A quiver ran through us, the prelude to collapse.

No, look at Sara. She's ready to fight. There's still time.

We slid down off of Charles' back. No one had noticed us yet. Z stood a few feet in front of Sara, tracing her shape in the air with a switchblade, like an artist ready to paint a portrait. We could see Tony in profile as he watched Z, panting heavily in the manner of a dog balancing a treat on its nose, waiting for permission from its master to eat. Jackson stared at his feet, ignoring everything else around him. They all looked so young.

Sara did not look at any of them. She was gazing past Z into the distance, across the Shelter. There, X sat alone on a bench, rocking and hugging his knees. He stared out into the distance away from the shelter, paying no mind to the blood that dripped from his nose and cut lip onto the torn fabric of his jeans.

All of them: stupid and young and dangerous.

We finally knew everything. Where everyone had been. What everyone had done. X's betrayal must have been devastating for Sara. That he would lead her to them, that he would sit by and do nothing. Sara never mentioned X—not to the police, not during the trial, not to any of us. In those days and weeks and months after the rape—after the physical wounds had healed, after the memories of the attack had mostly been repressed— she would have come to understand X's contrition more fully. The thought of it bubbling up to torment her. That was the wound that would never mend. But she kept their secret until her death. Sara's eyes bored into X, the boy she loved, the one she had decided to give herself to, and he refused to meet her gaze.

All of our fear, all of our resistance, disappeared. All of our wariness and mistrust, gone too. We were united with a single purpose. Together, in control. The mist of the Luminal was no match for our combined determination. We ate it up and gained strength from the adrenaline rush, a well-timed adverse reaction. Everyone in the room except Charles was high on something. Keyed up, we stepped forward. Charles stood by us.

"Enough fucking foreplay," Z said, lurching toward Sara. "Let's party."

Z tore the top out of her hands, revealing Sara's breasts to the night. The shirt hung around her waist like an apron.

"Get off me!"

"I don't think so," Z said, tickling her throat with the blade.

"Stop it!" Charles shouted.

Everyone turned toward us. Reflexively, Charles retreated a step as the three boys faced us down.

"Binky?" Sara said.

Her voice broke my heart.

"Sara," we said, tears flowing freely now.

No one moved. Z still held our sister at knifepoint.

"What the fuck are they doing here?" Z said.

Jackson finally focused, pulling back out of his head.

"Let's just go, man," Jackson said.

"Shut up, I'm thinking," Z said.

The thin layer of confidence he'd shellacked over his persona eroded under the elements, leaving the true Z revealed in all his twitchy uncertainty.

"Hold them," he said.

Tony was much faster than we expected. Charles tried to dart away, but too late, his reflexes not up to the task. Tony's hand was like an iron manacle on our small arm. Past his bulk, we could see Z reaching for his belt buckle. Sara tried to get up, but he nicked her throat with the blade and she stopped. We locked eyes with our sister.

"Just relax, darling," Z said, his voice wavering despite the bravado of his words. "This is what you wanted tonight, wasn't it?"

"I'm leaving," Jackson said.

"No one's going nowhere!"

But Jackson moved. That was his great offense. Taking that first step away from the railing toward the staircase. Jackson didn't even get his hands out of his pockets before Z drove his shoulder into the smaller boy's chest, sending him sprawling backwards, over the railing, and into space.

Tony laughed at of the sound of Jackson's body hitting the pavement below. Z leaned on the railing for a moment, looking down on his handiwork. We could hear Jackson whimpering in the distance.

The Luminal beckoned to us, offering a respite from what remained of this night. We pushed it aside. This was our chance. We bit down, hard and deep on Tony's hand, drawing blood. Then we were on the ground, head throbbing. He had hit us with his bloody knuckles.

"No!" Sara screamed. "Binky!"

"What the fuck are you doing?" Z said, spinning back toward the room.

"The kid bit me."

"Did I say to fucking hit him?"

"No, but—"

"You do what I say!"

It wasn't clear who Z was talking to. But everything had gone a little fuzzy. Maybe the Luminal had kicked back in—maybe we overestimated our resistance to the drugs. Maybe Tony hit us harder than we thought. But the room started to tilt a little. We tried to stand up and crumbled back to the ground.

Z had done the calculations in his head. He was past the point of no return. Crimes had been committed. There was no reason to stop now. He jumped Sara, knocking her onto her back, dropping his full weight on top of her.

X ran headlong into our field of vision. The flurry of activity that followed sent the Shelter spinning around us. X and Z tumbled off Sara, a single whirligig tumbleweed, struggling for the knife, rolling away. Tony moved to help Z, but Charles let out a battle cry worthy of the third-level fighter he always dreamed he might be. Our brother caught Tony off balance; the two of them fell away from us, down the stairs to the ground floor, out of sight.

"Binky. Please be okay."

Sara had found us. We had found her. We reached for sleep again as she wrapped us in her arms.

"Oh, Binky. You knew. How did you know?"

That was all she could say. We didn't need any more.

"Sara, go."

X's voice was weak, straining to speak one last time. Sara's hold on me loosened. We all saw them, Z straddling his brother, X grasping his brother's wrist, Z pushing the blade down toward his face, X losing.

"Go."

Sara pulled on our shoulder. But we shook her hand off. We could not trade Sara's rape for X's death. The ending could not be that neat, that simple.

Nothing was foretold. Nothing was determined.

"Now, Binky!"

Sara sounded like our mother, our father, Roger, Ms. Mittewag.

We refused to listen.

We ran at Z. He turned the knife toward us, more out of surprise than intent. He, like everyone, was surprised at the seven-year-old figure flying toward him, hands flailing, ready to strike aimlessly at the injustice of it all.

We saw it quite clearly. The knife pierced our palm and came through the other side of our hand. The pain cleaved us in two, separating us.

Binky's eyes rolled up into his head. I no longer had a window on the outside world. Inside the cave, the monstrous id howled and the resurgent superego retched. The Luminal mist retreated to the corners of the chamber, respecting our madness.

I was on fire. I could not find Binky within the inferno. Alone, engulfed in flames, I felt my flesh shrivel and char, desiccate and blow away.

This could not last, this pain. It could not.

And it did not.

We were no longer *we*.

I was gone.

TWENTY-FIVE

THE DARKNESS WAS complete. Yet I could see infinitely in all directions. It made no sense and I understood it absolutely.

This is where I was. There was no place else.

I was no longer inside Binky. This was my space and mine alone.

One arm dangled by my side. My arm. It did not move and I felt no need to move it. My other arm stretched out over my head, reaching for something above me. For no reason—this place had no use for reason—I looked up, searching for my hand. There it was, right where it should be. A thick knotted rope had been threaded through the hole in my hand, the place where Z had stabbed me, and now I realized that I was hanging here and that this rope was the only thing that tethered me to another world.

Another world. Another time. The past, the future, the present. None of that was clear. This was a place that defied explanation. It was absence, a true void, a lack. The nothingness embodied calm, and I was part of it. I felt nothing. Yet, here I was, still a consciousness, considering how I had come to be here, wondering what I was still connected to. There was no gravity to pull me in any particular direction. The rope held me, but did not exert any pressure on my hand. There was no pain.

I knew who I was. There was still an identity. I remembered the events I had experienced within Binky. But I found that everything that had come before and after eluded me. There were hazy memories. No, not memories—feelings. I knew there were people who loved me, people I loved. I knew I had hurt and been hurt. All of that swirled within me, searching for a foundation to attach to.

The problem was simple. And impossible. I lacked context. Whatever I was or had been or would be was in flux, reorganizing itself around me as I waited. I could feel the pieces shifting with me at their center.

It should have been terrifying, that uncertainty, but instead I felt only peace.

This is where I belonged. Where else would I be?

Somewhere else.

Of course, that was the only answer. This was nowhere. I belonged somewhere.

My mind cleared a bit.

The rope must lead somewhere. I tried to pull my bound hand toward me, but the rope was taut. No give at all. I was at the end of it. So instead I reached up with my free hand and grabbed hold of it. The fibers scratched at my uncallused palm. I relished the burn of it, the reality.

With ease, I pulled myself up level with my other hand. I was weightless. The air around—no, it was not air, the *space*—was frictionless. There was no resistance at all as I started hand over hand, climbing the rope, faster, faster, heading toward where I was supposed to be.

I didn't see the object fluttering down until it was almost on top of me. About the size of a poster, clearly two dimensional, it descended like an autumn leaf caught in the wind. Yet, when the flat side faced me, I could see depth within it, movement. A mechanized diorama, a scene in progress.

I stopped climbing and peered into it.

Missy O'Neill stared back out at me. She wore a pink, puffy-sleeved dress. She was older, a teenager. Missy smiled. A hand reached out for her. My hand holding a corsage. I pinned it to her dress.

It was a memory. It was *my* memory.

Something that hadn't happened. Then, it was within me and I knew that it had.

Missy had listened to Binky. We had become friends. She had never slept with Louis Kirk. She had never gotten pregnant. I took her to the senior prom and we spent all night laughing at the earnest couples who believed they were in love, who thought that that night meant forever.

I knew all of that in an instant. The memory had floated past me, out of sight, out of reach. I looked around. There were more of them appearing around me, some far out in the distance, some close enough to touch.

Another one rotated toward me. Inside, I saw a courtroom. Z sat next to a lawyer, looking cleaned up and slicked back in a newly purchased suit. From the witness stand, I held up my scarred hand, showing the jury where I had been stabbed. With my other hand, I pointed at Z.

Then that memory was out of sight as well. Suddenly I knew that Z and Anthony had been sentenced for the attack. Jackson had survived the fall, paralyzed from the waist down; he had testified as well.

I swiveled around just in time to catch a glimpse of my mother walking out of the house with the last of her suitcases. Conrad waited in his van. I watched her leave. I was ten years old.

That one twisted away, hiding the rest of the scene from my view.

The memories were everywhere now. The void had become

a roiling sea with wave after wave of memories falling around me. In countless numbers, they appeared.

In one, I saw myself in a dorm room with Charles. I must have been fourteen; he would have been twenty-one. I was there alone with him, visiting.

In the void, I laughed and cried. In the span of a few seconds, I had learned that my mother had abandoned me at a much younger age and that my brother had never abandoned me at all.

So much had changed. I could not process it all. I didn't understand why I couldn't find the memories inside me. They were mine, yet I didn't seem to own them.

Not yet.

I looked down. The memories were piling up below me, jumbled and disordered, overlapping and undecipherable. An entire life being recreated sheet by sheet.

My life.

I grabbed at the next memory that came within my grasp. It struggled against me, writhing to free itself from my hands, but I held tight and stared into it.

A cemetery. Mourners gathered around a freshly dug grave. A brilliant sunny day. I dreaded what I would find there. But I did not look away. I searched for Sara. But it wasn't her grave. Not this one. The headstone read Xavier Pascal. The memory refused to be held. It shuddered in my grip before lurching violently upwards and away from me, like a caught fish that wasn't quite dead. But I had held it long enough to know that X had killed himself and left a note apologizing for what he had done to Sara.

The trickle of memories turned into a blizzard. They beat at me as they fell past, too many now even to catch a moment inside them. Suddenly, the panic returned to me. As the memories disappeared into the morass just beyond my reach, I was overcome with the feeling that they might be lost to me forever. I needed to gather them all up, review each one, but I could barely focus my eyes with all the chaos around me.

I wanted to find Sara there. I could not.

If I didn't do something, I would lose her forever.

I forced myself to find my tethered hand, holding it in front of my face. I ignored the cacophony and grabbed the rope with my free hand. With a clean yank, I pulled it out, leaving only a gaping wound in my palm, which I hid within a clenched fist.

The rope slithered upward away from me, leaving me certain that I was never supposed to go in that direction.

Free, I fell backwards, down, into the collected memories below. They reached up for me and pulled me into them, embracing me and sharing all their secrets.

I woke up in a sweat, breathing heavily, the weight of all my history and all my actions pushing me down into the hospital bed. The room, blurry at first, slowly came into focus. It teemed with the whirs and buzzes and beeps that sustained me. The plastic tube snaked down my nose; the needle from the IV ripped into my arm, feeding me an unknown solution, drip by drip by drip.

I wondered what was real, what was imagined.

I was still here, in this hospital. The past was the past once again. And here, filled with drugs, just as my younger self had been, I had my own fog to contend with. I tried to remember, but there were so many empty spaces and blocked corridors.

I thought I was alone.

"You're awake," a familiar voice said. "Hi."

I turned my head, blinking through the filmy layer of sleep. I saw her sitting next to my bed. The young girl, the teenager I knew, the sister who I had last seen looking down on me as she cradled my head in her lap.

Sara.

I tried to speak. Words were hard to catch; they were butterflies flitting through my head.

"It's okay," she said. "They said the medication would make you a bit woozy."

She took my hand, this girl, and finally a word bubbled from a distant place into my mouth.

"Sara," I said.

My voice—finally my voice—echoed with Binky's youth.

"No," she said in a voice so confident and unsullied it made me ache. "Rachel."

Rachel? The name bounced around like a rubber ball in my mind, erratically and impossible to pin down. I didn't know anyone named Rachel.

"They said you'd be a little confused when you woke up," Rachel said. "Uncle Roger said to tell you to consider it a bad trip. You know how he is."

Rachel laughed. She couldn't have been more than fifteen, but she chuckled like an old soul who understood that certain things would never change and other things could not be counted on.

This girl was not Sara. I could see that now. She shared Sara's eyes, her nose, but there was something different in the mouth, the form of it. Her hair, slightly darker, less fine. But still, the most beautiful face I had ever seen.

"Rachel?"

"There you go. Welcome back. Do you want something? Are you thirsty?"

I managed to shake my head.

"Sara and Uncle Roger will be back in a few minutes. I made them go down to the cafeteria to eat something. We'll have to tell Sara you said her name first. You know she loves to be first."

Rachel rotated my hand palm up. It had never felt so good to move, to be contained within my own skin. There, between my third knuckle and my wrist, she traced a long scar, the place where Z had stabbed me.

"Sara is here?" I said. "My sister?"

I choked on my own saliva, sputtering out a weak series of

coughs. Rachel calmly brushed her fingers along my cheek and the tears in my throat came to my eyes.

"No, Uncle Ben, your daughter," she said.

"You look like her," I said. "So much like her."

I saw my own tears reflected in Rachel's eyes. My niece, Sara's daughter.

Then, forty pounds of pure energy hit me in the side. I flinched at the pain. My whole body a giant bruise.

"Daddy's awake!"

"Sara, don't," Roger said. "You'll hurt him."

"But he's awake!" Two small hands cupped my cheeks and turned my face toward hers. "Hi, Daddy!"

I looked into the smiling face of the girl I'd stranded in Guatemala. Here, now. Over her shoulder, Roger looked concerned and relieved.

"Sara?" I said, looking at Roger.

"I'm right here!"

"My sister?"

"I don't think he remembers me," Rachel said.

"It's okay," Roger said. "It's just the painkillers."

Roger sat down on the bed and took my free hand. Sara lay down on my chest, a comforting weight to bear.

"It's okay," Roger said. "But maybe next time you'll listen when I tell you not to try and clean out the gutters yourself."

"I fell?"

"You fell," Sara said, giggling.

And I knew everything. It all barreled into me at once. The aftermath of that night. My sister shaken but whole after the attempted rape. The divorce of my parents. Years of shuttling back and forth between my mother's home, which she shared with Conrad, and my father's apartment in the City, where he wrote and never published. Sara married and had a daughter. Then there had been an accident, and I had lost her again, dead on impact along with Rachel's father. My niece, an orphan at the age of one year. I took the girl in, and soon after that I met Roger, and we raised her together, an only child, until the day we decided to adopt. It was Roger's suggestion that our daughter be named Sara; he told me that as we stepped off the plane in Guatemala City. We moved to a house out in Greenwich, a perfect little family.

"Ben, maybe we should let you rest," Roger said. "Come on, girls, let's get some ice cream."

"No," I said. "Stay."

My family moved closer to me, surrounding me with their warmth. It had been so long since I had felt so secure. I did not want anyone to leave. I looked at Rachel.

"Rachel."

"You remember."

"Of course, I remember you," I said.

"And me?" demanded Sara.

"And you too," I said. "I remembered you first."

DISCUSSION QUESTIONS
FOR BOOK CLUBS

1. Would you consider Ben's family dysfunctional? Would you consider their problems to be connected to the way gender, divorce, and work were viewed in that time period? How might their situation have been different in the present?

2. Ben suffers from mental challenges such as panic attacks and obsessive-compulsive tendencies that appear to have been manifesting in Binky at an early age. To what extent do you think that Binky's problems contributed to the tension among the other family members? Again, would the situation have been different in the present?

3. The way Binky depicted himself and his family members in the drawing on the refrigerator foreshadows the future. Do you think, at such an early age, Binky already felt the distance between himself and his father? How about the rivalry with his brother?

4. Ben imparts wisdom on his younger self, though much of it, including tidbits about sex and dodgeball, is poorly received and ill-advised. If you could talk to your childhood self, what would you want to share? Do you think you'd listen to yourself?

5. How does Ben deal with his control issues, particularly when he has little control over his younger self?

6. How does Ben gain the trust of Binky?

7. Do you consider your older self as a different person from your younger self? Or do you see your life as a progression of different people?

8. Sara's ordeal was terrible, but unfortunately not unusual. Studies show that 1 in 6 women has been the victim of rape or attempted rape, and one-third of rape survivors contemplate suicide. How can we change this culture of sexual violence in our society?

9. How connected do you feel we are to our own pasts? Do you find that your own recollections shift over time?

MICHAEL LANDWEBER GREW up in Madison, WI, went to school in Princeton, NJ and Ann Arbor, MI, met his wife in Tokyo and currently lives with her and their two children in Washington, DC. He has worked at *The Japan Times*, the *Associated Press*, the U.S. Department of State, Partnership for a Secure America and the Small Business Administration. Mike is an Associate Editor at *Potomac Review* and a contributor on film and TV for *Pop Matters*. His short stories have appeared in places such as *Gargoyle*, *Barrelhouse*, *American Literary Review*, *Fugue*, *Fourteen Hills*, and *The MacGuffin*. You can find Mike online at mikelandweber.com. *We* is his first novel.

25741957R00114

Made in the USA
Lexington, KY
03 September 2013